Secrets

Unearthed

Part One

Chapter One

I could hear mutterings coming from the kitchen.

"Okay, I'm going… bye?"

I shouted to the suspicious looking closed door. Their voices went eerily quiet before my dad poked his head around the corner.

"Oh, Hi. Abby dear, I didn't hear you come downstairs."

My dad was acting weird.

"Yeah, just going to school. Don't you guys need to be at work?"

I asked curiously. It was my mum peering through the door now.

"You better hurry before you miss the bus darling."

She said before pulling my dad back into the kitchen.

I hurried to the bus just in time. I literally had to flag it down like a waving maniac. It took me a minute to catch my breath and find my seat. Here I was, on the bus again, same as I had been every school day this year. The big yellow bus stuck out like a sore thumb as it barrelled down the road.

I could backdate you with information of how my life was before this moment but I'll be honest I lived a fairly dull life before today. There's countless ways to begin a story,

4

yet there's only ever one way to end it. For this story I'll start in the middle, because that's where all the fun really begins.

I'd like to tell you that I had all the answers in life, including bullet points on how not to mess it up but that would be a lie. Life is messy, complicated, not to mention painful. I mean, is it making mistakes or is it just life lessons?

Either way, without the bad we would never appreciate the good. There are no shortcuts on how to get to adulthood. No matter how hard you try, there is no secret pathway leading us to become the best person we can be. You just have to surf the waves and pray you don't land belly up in the water.

Have you ever been surfing? Hitting the water after flying off your surfboard really hurts! Of course you never aim to fall off, but isn't that life through and through? No one ever sets out on this journey we call life intending to mess up their lives or hurt family members. I certainly didn't, I never saw it coming, yet when I look back it all makes so much sense.

Hindsight, a completely useless yet eye opening thing in life. I would say that if it was a game I'd be losing but my story isn't done yet so who knows what may come my way. All I can really be sure of in this moment is this; secrets are never a good thing. I'm sorry... where are my manners? You are probably wondering who the heck I am, right?

Well I'll tell you who I am, or at least who I was. In this moment of my life I'm a completely oblivious fourteen

©This work is copyrighted.

year old girl named Abigail Wilson. Also known as Abby amongst other hideous nicknames, so just call me Abby. How I long to be back on that bus, pretending both ear buds worked as I played my music. Life was so simple back then, not that I would have thought it at the time.

Today I had made an effort to wear my hair down, I'm not entirely sure why. I usually aim for a messy up-do for my long brunette hair. I can't abide my hair being separated from my head.

"No... no mr hairdresser I need that hair it is a part of me you know!?"

I had probably only had a handful of haircuts in my life, mostly because I'd been kicked out of every hairdresser within driving distance of us.

It is not my fault they can't handle criticism, although being called the worst hairdresser in the world by a six year old in front of a room full of potential customers can't be good for business. Come to think of it; watching a child scream bloody murder, almost as though a limb had been cut from her body as opposed to an inch of hair can't be a great way to advertise your business either. It went a little like this:

"Argh! Mum, make him stop! He's murdering my hair! ARGH!"

My mum eventually gave up and let me grow my hair mostly due to sheer embarrassment.

This plus the fact that I would shove it up before even running a brush through it leads to my stupendously chaotic lump of hair. In fact birds would happily nest in it and have tried to before. Enough about my outrageous hairstyle choices, what other important information should you know about me?

Okay, so my absolute favourite thing in the entire world is music, seriously could there be anything else better to pass the time with? Not for me, I could literally sing you the lyrics of any song in my playlist of a thousand random songs from memory. Trust me, people have tried to best me before but never succeeded. It's actually a great way to gain extra lunch money.

To be fair, I don't have much of a social life, I'm an only child with a total of one friend to claim as my own. I spend most of my time with my nose inside of a book with my music on full volume. Much to my mother's dismay; she always complains about the damage I'm doing to my ears. She may have a point but I would never give her the satisfaction of admitting that she was right. As a teenager my prerogative is to always give my parents a hard time, I'm sure you can relate.

Chapter Two

Here I was on the bus heading towards my impending doom. Sorry to be dramatic, but school and impending doom aren't far from each other. Today I was wearing my favourite ensemble of clothing which included baggy jeans with unintentional rips, a plaid shirt buttoned up only halfway which was draped over a plain white T-shirt and high-top sneakers worn in to perfection. Comfort is key when dealing with school, all you do is sit around all day 'learning' so there is no point in wearing my 'glad rags', now is there? Who was I going to impress?

All the boys at my school were either my shoulder height, king of the nerds or too cool for school. They definitely were not *my* type, not that I honestly knew what my 'type' was. Listening to music whilst enduring a boring bus ride was my best alternative. I heard a voice calling to me.

"Hey Abby, it's me Phil, saved you a seat."

It was 'Stinky Phil'. I *could* sit with him however I liked my nose so I really didn't want to offend it unnecessarily.

"I'm okay, but thank you."

I decided to gracefully decline his generous offer.

He was always talking about uninteresting topics of conversation. Today he was engrossed in his phone (playing some dumb game no doubt) he was wearing dilapidated brown shoes with navy blue corduroys, on his upper body was an equally depressing t-shirt; the label was so faded I couldn't make it out.

His boy band haircut was similar to something my dad would have shown off as a teen, it made him look as though he could be the lead in a seventies sitcom. Don't get me wrong, he was a lovely guy… *lovely* might be going a bit too far. He had a heart of gold buried under his dreadful appearance.

I normally have my bestie to chat with but Patricia was otherwise engaged, she was smooching with Tyler (her latest flavour of the month).

"Hey Patz, Tyler."

I greeted them as I tried to hide my jealousy. I didn't like Tyler much, mostly because he monopolised my best friends' time.

One thing he had going for him was his luscious locks. The boy had the coolest hair, it just begged for you to ask a question like **'What shampoo do you use?'** or **'What is this secret to that shine?'** there had to be some elusive formula he used in order to obtain its bounce! They were wearing matching outfits today as if it were on purpose, although it was purely accidental most of the time.

Last Christmas they both wore these hideous handmade, coarse woollen jumpers featuring one saying **'HAPPY'** and the other saying **'HOLIDAYS'**. They spent all day walking around in the right order so as not to confuse people. Patricia's Nana knitted it for them, she had used the word 'holidays' so that it could be politically correct. This was in order for it not to offend anyone's beliefs (leaving no excuses for not wearing it), unfortunately for the 'lovestruck' pair of teenagers.

This time Tyler was modelling a beige cashmere jumper, smart black jeans with matching ebony shoes. Patricia stood wearing a jet-black cashmere jumper, beige cropped jeans and tan shoes.

"Did you plan those outfits? You look just like a chess set."

I teased gently. Patricia just poked her tongue out at me before sticking it back down Tyler's throat.

I spent the day squinting at them because when I did they resembled my kitchen tiles, however they did not find my teasing humorous. Up close these two could easily pass for a married couple, like two pieces of a jigsaw puzzle they just fitted together. Their comparable golden hair meant blonde babies without a doubt, seeing them together made me believe that Patricia had finally met 'the one'.

Those piercing blue eyes of his were completely loved up staring into her doe hazel eyes, as if they were the only two humans left on earth. I envied them slightly, not because I wanted her boyfriend but because I wanted her life. I'd have happily traded places, she seemed to have it made. It wasn't just me, those two love birds would bring out the green-eyed monster in most people. They were the envy of the school.

I hadn't met a guy that I had found interesting enough to have a relationship with (yet), I was waiting for Mr. Right. There was gossip floating around the school that I batted for the other team (untrue of course). I just shrugged it off, school was so close to being over for the summer break; I just knew my guy had to be in college. I needed an intellectual guy, smarter than he appeared, amongst his many admirable traits would be the fact that he was humble. My biggest turn off was an arrogant guy that just knew he was God's gift to women.

I had my entire life planned out, right down to the design on my wedding china. I could see it playing out like this: I would be at a frat party reading a thick book in the corner, ironically of course, when the man of my dreams would sit down next to me and give me a reason to put the oversized piece of literature down. We'd kiss, get married, have babies then get a house in the suburbs; white picket fence, the whole shebang. As unrealistic as it sounds, the dream was my best kept hidden secret.

Chapter Three

Oh my, sorry, I do get carried away in a whirlwind of thoughts and imagination. Where was I? Secrets are bad, right? Well let's set the scene first, we'll get to the juicy bits soon enough. Today was the day my life flipped upside down! I remember it as if it were yesterday. The bus was at a standstill, we were stuck in traffic yet again. The sound of horns blaring polluted my ears as it sliced through the smooth jazz song I was playing. Yes I like smooth jazz, amongst many other music genres. Don't knock it till you've tried it.

You could cut through the tension in the air just as you would a chunk of cheddar cheese. My playlist always kept me upbeat, I liked so many different types of music. When I put it on shuffle it could go from country to pop then slip back into some rock and roll. I never knew what to expect but was usually pleasantly surprised. Even with my songs playing I couldn't escape the mutual frustration felt by all, gruelling conversations about traffic and how awful it was surrounded me.

Our bus driver was grumbling under his breath as per usual, I could hear mutterings of how his life would be different had he won that battle of the bands concert back in the day. He continued on to say how Stuart the drummer had ruined his life by not showing up when he needed him most.

"Damn you Stuart!"

He said quite loudly, he was clearly fed up with his job.

I definitely needed better headphones, the broken side was being used purely as decoration. As much as I tried to drown out the world I couldn't, I heard way more than I wanted to. It is amazing what you can learn about a person when they think you aren't listening.

Actually that reminds me of one Thanksgiving when my cousin Heather Miller came to stay, just saying her name sends shudders down my spine. The prima donna was always talking on her cell phone at night with her 'so say' secret boyfriend. She thought I was asleep as I was 'lame' in her eyes and couldn't handle the late nights, in Chicago she would stay up past midnight; a fact she constantly reminded me of. The truth was that I just didn't like her (in case you hadn't already figured that one out on your own), her snotty attitude was too much for me to cope with.

She was a whole five feet four inches of phoney, but besides how much I hated her, I had to admit that she had a fierce look. The girl had the cutest button nose which meant her face was the picture of your typical 'girl next door'. Her short bob of chocolate mousse coloured hair taunted me every time I laid eyes on her; I was certain that she had to be adopted.

We were cut from a different cloth for sure, complete opposites. So when I learnt about this delicious new information I decided that it was in my best interests to keep it to myself until an opportune moment had arrived. Thankfully it wasn't long before I got my perfect opportunity to reveal the juicy gossip I had acquired.

I managed to cleverly sneak the tasty morsel into the conversation while we were all sitting around the dinner table, it was decorated to the nines. Our plates were laden with turkey featuring all of the trimmings, seasonal Thanksgiving décor surrounding us with an equally festive atmosphere. We were going around the table saying what had made us thankful this year, it had reached my turn when 'little miss know it all' decided to pipe up. I know what you're thinking… it wasn't my information to tell and perhaps I should learn to be a little less petty, right?

Trust me you would have done exactly the same in my position. Don't believe me? Just listen to what she said but imagine it in a horribly insincere way.

"I just want to say how grateful I am for such thoughtful parents, thanks for bringing me here to Aunt Deedee and Uncle Billie's *amazing* Thanksgiving! I wouldn't trade you guys for *all* the money in the world, there is literally no place I'd rather be or in the company of anyone else at this time of year. So this year I am thankful for *all* of my family."

Her smirk spoke for itself, like she was fooling anyone! Well actually she was fooling *everyone*, that's why I had to do it. So I did do it... but I'm getting ahead of myself.

Her speech was a little over the top if you ask me, that is the nicest way of describing it too. Heather always called my parents those stupid nicknames, their names were Deidre and William not Deedee and Billie! Literally no one else called them that, of course my parents thought it was endearing... *gross*. I got ready to ruin the day of 'Princess up herself'; I cleared my throat.

"I thought you would be most grateful for your 'snuggle wump' Benjamin whom you *utterly* adore, you know the one you converse with every night *incognito*."

I had to dodge a napkin thrown in my direction but it was totally worth it, I think the posh yet 'cutesy' baby voice I said it in had tipped her over the edge.

I remember relishing the moment where she pleaded with her parents that I was lying yet getting nowhere. My parents however did not see things my way. We were both grounded for a month and she still refers to me as her annoying Cousin 'Gail the whale' (mostly because it rhymed) whom she hates, but at least she doesn't make Speeches anymore; one annoying Thanksgiving tradition down just Christmas still to conquer!

My bitter sweet victory didn't seem to stop her getting everything she wanted in life. I seemed to be surrounded by perfect girls with perfect lives. I was more of an odd duck than anything else, I didn't seem to fit in anywhere, even with my friends and family. Especially with my family.

Chapter Four

Sorry for the information overload, it's all relevant to the upcoming events. There are a lot of people in this story so try to keep up. I hope you're not thinking it's just teenage drama coming my way, I assure you it's far worse. Where was I... ah, yes, I remember. The day my whole life changed irrevocably.

I keep coming back to this moment on the bus, I know it seems like I've been sitting on this stinking bus for hours. To be honest it felt like hours at the time and all these thoughts pass through my mind every time I'm taken back there. It was just so odd, today seemed to be just like any other day, I must have replayed every moment back in my head just to make sure I didn't miss any obvious clues that today was the day my entire life was going to transform from bland to crazy.

The bus finally reached school a full twenty minutes late. By the time we had entered the school gates I was just about able to pry Patricia away from Tyler.

"Isn't he *so* dreamy big Gail."

Patricia sighed out loud. To briefly explain the name 'big Gail', it was Patricia's unique nickname for me, I wasn't exactly going to be called 'small Gail' seeing as my sheer size doubled Patricia's.

It was in height however more than girth, I was five feet six inches tall with broad shoulders. On top of that I was sporting quite a manly figure without much on the 'curve side' of life. Patricia was a pint size flawless human with luscious hair that hung down in shiny curls. I didn't mind the nickname, but only when she said it. Tyler tried to call me big Gail once but never again, I think he feared my 'don't even think about it' glare.

"Yes Patricia, he is so dreamy that I can barely stay awake while in his presence!"

I gave her a sarcastic look so she wouldn't think badly of me.

She giggled in her sweet innocent way then began to tell me all about her plans to become Mrs. Tyler Johnson. It was adorable really, they made an idyllic couple, on top of never arguing they shared the same dumb passion for eating raspberries dipped in mango yoghurt. What could possibly go wrong?

"Okay Patricia, I get it, he is so perfect that he must secretly be a demiGod, but tell me just one thing..."

Patricia's curious gaze made me want to laugh. I stifled my giggles as I continued with my question.

"...did he tell you the secret formula for the bounce in that hair of his!?"

I hardened the features on my face to make her think that I was being deadly serious.

I should honestly be a famous actress by now; my talents are wasted in Midtown High.

"Oh! Big Gail, you do love to tease me, don't you!"

We laughed before heading off to class in order to face *Mr. Rat.* He wasn't a real rat he just mirrored one, his face was screwed up with glasses way too big for his face held up by the severe point to his enormous nose. His name was actually Mr. Richardson, but for the purposes of the story we shall refer to him henceforth as Mr. Rat. He was waiting impatiently, he was clasping tightly to a large stick of chalk whilst tapping his foot.

Mr. Rat was looking particularly rodent like today, he also seemed to be in a foul mood.

"Abigail Wilson and Patricia Moore I should've guessed that *you* two would be the last ones into class."

He snarled as his arms folded around his scrawny body. The Rat smirked quite wickedly like he knew an inside joke that none of us were privy to.

"Sorry Sir."

Patricia and I chimed in unison.

"The bus was late."

I added. We shuffled towards our chairs with our heads as low as the ground.

His smirk immediately left his face as he spoke in a low tone.

"Yes well, I suppose that couldn't be helped."

Mr Rat seemed to be a little bit disappointed by the fact that he couldn't tell us off for being late, considering it was because of factors beyond our control.

He continued with the lesson as soon as our bums hit the chairs so I got comfortable as I allowed my mind to wander. He would only bore me if I listened to his droll tone about whatever it was that he was trying to teach us about today. In all fairness I could get an A in my sleep. Our exams were a week away now, I had studied enough to last me a lifetime, so I figured that if I put a few more hours in over the weekend I would be just fine.

Chapter Five

As my mind hopped on a train and left the station I started to think about the morning's events, in particular a conversation I hadn't been invited to join. I'd overheard my parents talking about something. Not much to go on, I know. Their voices were very muffled, even though I couldn't make out all of the words that were being said, I definitely heard my name being mentioned including something to do with the fact that they were worried about how I would handle 'it'; whatever 'it' was.

My parents were decent folk (as far as I knew), they had led a fairly quiet life without too much excitement. Although they never really discussed anything in their lives prior to my birth. My mother Deidre was a simple woman who wore a lot of puce coloured clothing with minimal accessories, on the other hand my father William was a stout man who loved gaudy shirts which he would wear alongside a variety of patterned clothing items; clashing clothes was his forte.

They seemed to be complete opposites yet they never fought about the big things, they did however argue often about trivial things; such as not putting the toilet seat down or over whose turn it was to do the dishes. They shared the same hazelnut colouring to their hair which matched mine perfectly; we were like three peas in a pod from the outside looking in. I bet you're wondering about that comment I made about not fitting in with my own family. True we didn't have many problems, I just have always felt a weird distance between us.

It was almost as though I was a guest in my own home; a bystander to my own life. Our relationship was only ever surface deep. They were great for what I needed but never for what I felt I wanted. I love them, but they kept me out of the loop of anything that held importance. Like this morning's conversation; I knew I couldn't butt in and expect answers. Instead I pretended all is fine in the world.

We had lived in the same house in Atlanta for as long as I could remember, I had fond memories of trips to the local park while my parents played the 'One, Two, Three... weeee' game as I like to call it; they would each hold an arm of mine then raise me into the air on the number three whilst swinging me forward a few steps. To me it was the most exhilarating game but to them it was just their way to speed up my walking. I found this out late in life when we had a discussion about it.

The house itself didn't exactly impress on first sight, there was however a certain charm to its tired walls along with the mild décor. My favourite thing about it had to be the attic, it was the perfect size for building a fort. I would love pretending I was a princess trapped in a tower awaiting the rescue from a handsome knight; being a kid was a time I missed dreadfully.

There was no end to the places my imagination could take me to, one day I would be in China eating noodles and the next day I would be on a gondola in Italy. It was a regular detached house which included an unkempt surrounding garden, our house appeared to be 'out of place' in the street; stood amongst such decorated homes was our misshapen, awkward abode. Our neighbours were equally friendly as they were quiet, they mostly kept to themselves just as we did.

Chapter Six

My imagination could be my best friend or my worst nightmare, at that moment in time it was doing more harm than good. I'd often let it run away from me; before I knew it I'd be thinking of worst case scenarios. As much as their private conversation bothered me I wasn't going to be the one to bring it up.

Our family policy was to keep smiling and it would all be fine; we basically never talked about our feelings. My first thought immediately landed on the possibility that they were getting divorced or that one of them may be dying.

I had to remind myself that my parents were a rock, I'm sure they wouldn't quit just like that, besides no illness could beat them. Wishful thinking perhaps, but I had always been the designated dreamer in my family. I'd like to think that someday I'll have my own family, which will include grandparents for my children.

I never had the chance to meet my grandparents before they died. All I wanted in life was to have a great big family so that our Christmases together were never dull. Unlike every Christmas I had endured with that 'miss perfect' cousin of mine, my dream didn't include her being in the picture.

I could see it as if it was happening right now, I'd take young Molly and Mike to go see Granny and Gramps. Their eyes would light up when they unwrapped their presents, I would hold my husband's hand thinking how lucky could a girl get. Patsie would have her family visit often, we would have the fanciest barbecues known to man. We'd idly gossip with a glass of wine in our hands whilst watching our men burn the meat on the hot charcoal and drinking beer.

I had a grand plan for my life, I didn't need any crazy dramas interfering with it. Just the idea of two homes sent a worrisome chill down my spine. A classmate of mine at school has just been through a horrid time with their parents divorce. As much as having two birthday parties would seem like fun, it really wasn't, especially when only half of your family and friends were at each one.

As parents went I lucked out, they tried hard to be just the right amount of concerned but not too involved so as not to alienate me. They let me stay up late to finish the end of a film, or finish my chapter in the book I was reading even when it ran past my bedtime. I also got to see or message my friends whenever I needed to, so long as I didn't break curfew.

Not that I had many friends, or invites to leave my house past eleven at night. Patsie's parents were as strict as they come, she had to be home week nights whilst only being allowed out at the weekend for a few hours at a time. I was allowed over but had to leave by eight o'clock at night as she had to complete her set tasks for the day before bed.

I truly felt for her, that's why I let her off for spending so much time with her boyfriend during school hours. Boy time wasn't seen as a relevant way to pass the time in her house, she would often lie by saying she was seeing me just to see him at the weekend. She would come to my house and I would tell my parents we wanted to go to the mall which was code for her going on a date and me amusing myself.

She did try to set me up with one of his friends but that didn't go down well. I just ended up playing in the arcade while I waited for her to finish smooching her hunky man. I didn't let my loneliness phase me, I didn't need a boy to give me purpose.

My decision to become a Doctor when I grew up was the thing that drove me to study hard, I wanted to save people's lives or do some good in the world. I know it wasn't an easy path to take, I would have to keep hitting the books as well as keeping my grades up but it was my dream. Plus when I was this awesome doctor I would have no trouble finding a man to share my life with, right?

When I get home I am certain that my parents will be back to their happy selves. I would come home to my mum gently teasing my dad about the parrots on his shirt, saying that they had been eyeballing her for the whole day. To be fair those parrots did eyeball anyone who looked their way. My mum had tried to donate the shirt to charity many times; unsuccessfully.

Chapter Seven

School went past in a blur just as it usually did, nothing unexpected happened, unless you count Tyler catching a peanut in his mouth after three tries! It was far better than the previous day; it took him a total of five tries instead (yeah, I wasn't that impressed either). The enjoyment of my school day ebbed away as I arrived home to find my mum, face first in the palms of her hands.

She was at the kitchen table; my dad was trying to console her however he seemed to be doing a poor job of it.

"Mum are you okay? Did Dad burn the meatballs again?"

I tried to integrate some humour into the situation, I had made it my mission in life to always see positivity in all of life's dramas.

I suppose you would like me to explain the basis of my joke... no? Well I will anyway... there was an incident that happened while my dad was in charge of dinner. I was only twelve at the time, my mum had to go away on a business trip. She was going to be gone until late into the evening. She left explicit instructions on how to reheat the meatballs (her cooking from the previous night).

Even a baby could have done it, not my dad however! He managed to set the microwave on fire and burn the meatballs to a crisp. He had only gone and left the aluminium foil around the dish. This is what he said to defend himself:

"I didn't know I couldn't cook the tin foil! It just said to place in the microwave."

He'd held up my mum's list of instructions in defence.

After I took a look at it I felt the need to point out that he had gotten meatball sauce over the list; the first point did say to remove the tin foil. We both looked at the dish containing charcoal that had originally been intended for our dinner. It had been rendered inedible so we had to order take away instead. My mum of course was furious because even a monkey would know that metal plus microwaves equaled explosions (her words, not mine). Anger turned to laughter and it forever went down in history as one of dad's greatest mess ups.

We ended up buying a new microwave for his birthday and affixed a note that is still there saying please don't put tin foil inside as I might explode. I had hoped this memory would have been enough to bring back their smiling faces.

Instead I received two faces looking in my direction with forced smiles on their faces, I could see a great sadness in their eyes.

"Sit down Abby, we have something important to discuss..."

My mother's pale face had a pink hue around her eyes where she had been clearly crying. She gestured for me to sit while my dad pulled the chair out for me. As I sat down into the chair my father squeezed my shoulders lovingly, the seat now felt as though it had been turned into stone. I couldn't get comfortable.

My dad sat down next to my mum as I became pensive, what could this news be? Would they get a divorce? Was I adopted? Were we from outer space? Yeah that might be a stretch, but still.

Chapter Eight

So many thoughts raced around in my mind, I can't even tell you what they were. I was in a confused state until my worrisome thoughts were interrupted abruptly by a shaky voice.

"Your grandma Jean is extremely unwell, we had hoped this day would never come, nevertheless it's our duty to look after her in her hour of need..."

As my father continued he cleared his throat, my face had changed into a mess of confusion. I didn't have a grandma.

Anytime I'd brought up grandparents as a child the topic was changed. The only thing that had ever been said was that they were no longer with us. So you can understand why I'd think they were all dead and buried.

"...you won't know this but we were born and raised in Kent, a place in England. We chose to move out here for a better life. Your grandma Jean is Deidre's mum... Well... Um... You see..."

My face had turned from confusion into sheer horror at this stage which had put my dad on the spot a little bit, moreover it seemed to leave him fumbling for words whilst failing miserably. My mum placed her hand upon my dad's shoulders to silence him, for which he was grateful for.

As my mother continued from where my dad had left off, she began to tell me about this Grandma I had never heard of before. It seemed they didn't get along due to the fact that she was against my parents marriage or some such drama. I had lost interest in the story she was telling me, I was more concerned with the fact that I had been kept completely in the dark for my entire life. I folded my arms crossly.

"So, how is this my problem? Why tell me now if you were so keen on keeping it a secret all of these years? Can't you just fly off to wherever she lives?"

They shook their heads simultaneously.

With continued determination I pleaded my case

"You can leave me here until you come back, I can stay with Patricia..."

My mother's tone became sharp while she cut me off mid sentence

"No Abigail, that wouldn't be an option in this case, your grandmother has insisted on you being there, we owe her this much at least."

They owed her? How was that my problem? Besides what about owing me? I sat there while fury bubbled up inside of me.

"You might owe her but I don't! I'm not going!"

After a short pause to look at each other they told me the worst news I had ever received in my entire life.

"We will be gone for the summer, if not longer, there is no other option here. Sorry."

I practically screamed out loud for my next sentence.

"WHAT!? What about *me*? I have friends here, people who 'get me'! I can't just make *new* friends! What would *I* do for the whole summer!?"

My mother shrugged seemingly unaffected by my outburst of rage.

"I'm sure we will find something for you to do Abigail."

I stormed off leaving the chair slapping on the ground as I exited the room.

"ARGH!"

How dare they completely ruin my life like this!?

Chapter Nine

With so many different things to be concerned about I didn't know where to start. I was English? Do I like drinking tea now or eating cucumber sandwiches? Worst of all, I was going to be separated from my closest friend who I shared everything with. I couldn't believe they were being so selfish and what liars! Who do they think they are? I was beside myself with grief, I had absolutely not a clue how to break the news to Patricia. Who even was I?

I had so many unanswered questions that left me feeling perplexed. I threw myself onto my neatly made bed (instantly making it messy), I covered my face with my hands as I laid there feeling sorry for myself. Try as I might to see a way out of this, I couldn't. My imagination had finally failed me. I had no choice but to give my closest friend in the whole world the unfortunate news.

After much pacing I gazed upon my now thinning carpet, feeling sorry for its lack of lustre I began staring at the specs of dirt before me. It was as though the differing colours, shapes and sizes had me mesmerised. I kept thinking I should get the hoover out yet didn't have the willpower to get up and do it.

My anger had already dissipated after having the chance to think things through. My parents must have had a good reason for abandoning their home so suddenly, they weren't in favour of rash decisions normally. I stood up with purpose as I travelled downstairs.

I had every intention to apologise for my behaviour and hear them out, that was until I overheard my mother's phone conversation. She was on the phone with Grandma Jean, so I crept into the kitchen. I heard some of the conversation; my mum was reassuring the old dear that I was really looking forward to visiting her and couldn't wait to visit England (yeah right).

I had a choice to make, do I storm back upstairs or confront her? I had never had an argument with my parents before today so I had no clue on how to proceed. I decided to make light of the situation rather than cause a fuss. Playing the clown was my best job in this family.

I deliberately cleared my throat, this caused poor Deidre to jump out of her skin, shrieking at the top of her lungs. A grin took over my face as she fumbled for the words in order to try and explain herself.

"It was a mouse mum, so sorry I have to go... I will call you later, love you...Bye!"

She quickly hung up the phone before I could do anything else to trouble her.

"Abby you scared me!"

I folded my arms and wagged my index finger at her.

"Now Mother, you know you shouldn't lie to those you care about, it could lead to unexpected *surprises*."

I giggled quietly to myself feeling triumphant.

It took her more than a minute to see the funny side of my prank. Her panic had transformed into amusement as she chuckled softly.

"So have you decided to calm down now? Will you let me explain to you..."

I raised my hand to interrupt her intentionally, in jest.

"I will hear you out, I also forgive you for the secrets, you don't normally lie so I figure there must be a good reason behind it all. Am I right?"

Her disapproving gaze at my hand gesture led me to simper sheepishly. Clearly she was no longer in the mood good ole Abby the jester.

After a small pause my mother replied.

"*You* are my reason Abigail, I wanted to be with your father however my mother was not going to allow that. She wanted to send me away to a convent, that way I could have the baby in secret. Her plan was to raise you as her own, I simply couldn't go through with it. Your father came to the conclusion that we should elope and I agreed."

I feigned shock before letting her continue.

I managed to get half a smile for my efforts.

"William's sister lived in Chicago so they helped us move here."

I furrowed my brow for a mere moment then crinkled my nose with a cheeky expression.

"Well I am a pretty good reason, aren't I?"

My mother looked as if the weight of the world had lifted than she squeezed me tighter than she ever had before.

"OK, Mum, let me breathe...*Please.*"

I spoke with the little breath that I had spare, she then released me so I continued.

"Just please promise me that it is only temporary, we will come back home won't we? *Pretty please, with a cherry on top?*"

I held my hands as if I were getting ready to pray whilst I used a tone of voice that showed the utmost desperation, she nodded in agreement while finding my display very amusing.

Chapter Ten

With one problem now sorted I headed back upstairs. My laptop was calling to me, I had spent enough time in the real world as it was. Patricia would be my next challenge to face. How was I going to convince her firstly to visit me in England and secondly forgive me for abandoning her? She had never even left Atlanta before now, let alone travel to a whole other continent. I was due to log online to talk with her any moment now.

I felt a golf ball sized lump in my throat as I logged into our private online chat room. Each click of the keys on my keyboard was like a singular drum beat. Her username had a green dot next to it which meant she was already waiting for me, before the next second had passed a message from Patricia had already chimed through.

This was how our conversation went:

PATZIE<3 TYLER 4va

HEY BESTIE

GAIL :¬P

Hi Patz, got some bad news... I'm going to be a bit far away for this summer holiday...a *lot* far away...

PATZIE<3 TYLER 4va

OMG Where are you going? On Holiday? Without me!? :¬[

Gail :¬P

Not a holiday but I'll be in England... :¬(

PATZIE<3 TYLER 4va

Calling you NOW!

True to her words Patricia rang that instant, I was still reading her last message when my phone started buzzing uncontrollably.

I answered with dread knowing that once I had told her the full story she too would be as sad as I was. The conversation went on for over an hour, I caught her up on all of the 'ins and outs' of the why, the how and the when; I included all that I'd learned so far.

She made me promise to keep our online chats going every night without giving her any excuses, it was helpful to be able to share this startling new revelation that I was now dealing with. Patricia was my rock and even though she had been busier since meeting Tyler she still tried her best to make time for me.

I have to admit, it might be interesting to visit another country; although I can't think of what there would be to amuse me in Kent let alone with some dithering, old lady bothering me. I resolved to do some research online just so I knew what to expect upon my arrival. My search engine was now filled with such drab and dreary images, there were so many castles in the vicinity.

How many castles do you need to visit in one lifetime? Once you have seen one cold, damp stone building you have seen them all, am I right? The computer information began to depress me so I went back to reading my make-believe fictional stories, at least they had happy endings! It was either that or study, I can't believe I'm even considering hitting the books, that is how bad things were at this moment in time.

Chapter Eleven

School on Monday was going to be awkward to say the least; knowing I was leaving, on top of it being exam week wasn't ideal. The dynamic between us had changed, there was a noticeable strain on my relationship with Patricia. She was saying and doing all the right things but I knew deep down she was unhappy about it.

There had been an ever-growing distance between us since I told her the news of my upcoming departure, every time we spoke recently it had become pleasantries and idle chatter, instead of anything heartfelt or meaningful. To the outside world nothing had changed, yet I couldn't shake this feeling that I was losing her.

Fond summer memories washed over me, back then it was a simpler time. We would take a trip to the lake-house together, her family owned the place and my family had been invited to join each year since we met. I sat grinning whilst thinking about our time spent together sharing hotdogs, burgers and a couple of fizzy drinks with tropical style ice cubes floating inside. Come on, ice shaped as pineapples floating in a virgin Pina colada, what else in life could be better than that?

I didn't think anything was wrong with how our summer's were being spent at the time. That was until Tyler's family came to join us, I am all for the saying more the merrier however I didn't like how much it changed the atmosphere. It went from being gal pals enjoying the summer to girlfriend and boyfriend 'macking' on each other. My feelings ranged from awkward at best to the last one picked for a dodgeball match at worst.

It was last year the boy wonder joined us with his family, they were even more high end than Patricia's. I guess they had been slumming it when spending time with us, either that or felt they should lower themselves to our level in order to help us fit in. All I know is that the food changed from rustic barbecue into tiny appetisers I couldn't even pronounce the name of.

Tyler's family were like poodles, Patrica's were shih-tzus leaving us (the pit-bulls) feeling out of place. Not a pretty picture, I know who I would back in a dog show. I mean even a suit wearing pit-bull is still a pit-bull at the end of the day.

I had never noticed the class difference between us before, I felt as if I had belonged in her world, that was until Tyler made it very clear how wrong I was. I was like a third wheel to their perfect bicycle, or a stabiliser wheel after you already could ride without it. Having a boyfriend is all well and good but you can never talk to them about everything going on in your life.

Who would want to tell their boyfriend about what top looks cutest with the blue trousers you love wearing; I certainly wouldn't. I didn't see the appeal to it all or maybe I just hadn't met anyone who gave me those butterflies in my tummy, that feeling you read about in novels but never seem to experience for yourself.

There was a boy who asked me out once (well I think he did anyway), I was in the park walking my old dog Scruffles. The old timer was my best friend but has since passed away, he was being rehomed when he was sixteen years old, we found him at the pound where he was actually due to be destroyed if nobody claimed him as theirs. He had been there for a while, unloved and unwanted, the look in his eyes just killed me inside as I walked past him. It was love at first sight, his scruffy fur gained his name Scruffles; I just had to have him.

I couldn't let him be put down, his tiny eyes had peered into my soul. My parents had promised me any dog of my choice for a birthday present. They had spent all morning convincing me it was better to rehome a dog as opposed to buying a puppy, so they couldn't say no when I asked them for Scruffles. I thought about changing his name but it fit him so well; he was so loving. He would follow me anywhere I went, despite my parents initial protests he ended up staying in my bed at night.

I often took him out to my local park for his walk but today he wasn't feeling very energetic. I was sitting on a park bench when a boy came over to me from the other side of the park, he began saying how much he liked my dog and how we should go on a dog walk together.

It was a bit odd but I went with it, we arranged a time and a place however before our planned outing Scruffles got sick, I forgot all about the boy until weeks later but never saw him again. We had to put poor old Scruffles down but I convinced myself he had gone to a better place. We had a funeral in our garden and marked the spot with a hand-crafted head stone.

Other than that uninspiring incident no real interest had been shown in me, Patricia on the other hand had plenty of guys to choose from; she had them eating out of the palm of her hands. Maybe it was her tiny size or her 'innocent act' that she had mastered over the years, either way the boys loved her and often used me to get to her. There was just one time when I really liked a boy at school, when he finally came to talk to me it was only to find out if Patricia would go out with him.

I gave up shortly after that and stuck to what I knew I could control, which were my books. I loved reading interesting stories about these women who seemed to have it all, I loved reading their stories filled with confidence. They knew just how to get what they wanted out of life, using their feminine wiles to get to exactly where they needed to be. I would often get lost in my own little world of imagination, I'd start pretending to be these women of wonder, it was much better than accepting my lot in life.

I endured a lonely bus ride due to Patricia's absence from my journey into school, I was looking forward to seeing her beaming face as I entered into the gates where she normally would be waiting after her lift in. Again, I saw nobody, not in my classes nor throughout the day either. Mr. Rat was nicer to me than he usually was which was potentially out of pity, he probably empathised with my loneliness.

I spent the duration of the day concerned that she had to be unwell, maybe even on her deathbed... that was until my fears were put to rest by a text. The conversation read as follows:

PATRICIA:

Hey big Gail soz 2 B a pain but cld U keep notes 4 me 2day & 2moro. Feel free 2 do the homework 4 me :¬D

ME:

Sure thing did U catch mono again :¬P

PATRICIA:

Gross... no reminders plz... no.... Xplain L8R

ME:

COOL B¬). I hope UR OK?

Delivered

I now knew that she was clearly not dead, however a new mystery had now arrived as to why she wasn't in today and also wouldn't be tomorrow either, she was never normally this cagey about why she wasn't in school.

I guess I just had to wait until seven o'clock tonight to find out what on earth was going on, she always logged on at the same time every night to catch up with me, I knew it had to be something pretty serious to miss school but I was clueless as to what it could be.

I slinked into the house and put my school things in the hallway cupboard, my parents were home early again, I could hear their hushed tones coming from the master bedroom. Was this now my new normal? I already didn't like this grandma of mine, she was changing everything for the worse.

Chapter Twelve

It was my turn to cook dinner which basically meant I picked my favourite dinner that Mum had cooked from the freezer, so today I was going for an all-time comfort food 'mac, bac n cheese', my mum made the best mac n cheese using four different types of cheeses with crispy bacon then baked it in the oven.

So, I set the table then I sat down to eat what had to be my best reheating skills to date, I began waiting for my parents to join me but they never came. I ate my share and covered the others with aluminium foil, it seemed nobody had interest in talking to me today; I skulked off to my room in order to do my homework and waited for

Patricia to appear online. I finally gave up and went to bed by nine, the red blob next to PATZIE<3 TYLER 4va was majorly getting me down.

I chose fantasy over reality as I dove into one of my favourite novels, I had read it so many times before, the book had become so weathered that some of it's pages were actually trying to make their escape, it was my go to book when the reality of life was a little too much to cope with. The ladies in my books never let me down (unlike in real life), the time had reached past ten before my parents reared their guilt-ridden faces through my door.

They both shared a shamefaced gleam in their expression as I raised my eyes to meet theirs.

"I enjoyed *my* dinner at least, I suspect yours was a little cold by the time you got to it"

I said as I returned to my book with strong intentions of ignoring them.

"We are very sorry Abby, we were arranging the travel plans for our trip to England, there is a lot to do in such a short space of time. We lost track of the time... we noticed your light on and thought we'd come in to apologise."

I hated it when my dad spoke for both of them, they were forever keeping up a united front.

Mum sauntered across the room leaving my dad standing idle before sitting down beside me.

"Your Dad is completely right Hun we are so *sorry*; did you have a bad day? You seem a little down."

I gave up ignoring them as it was clearly no use, I closed my book as tears filled my eyes, my mum pulled me in for a big hug.

It wasn't long before my dad ran over hurriedly to join us; this made me giggle the tears away.

"I'm okay, you guys. I just didn't have anyone to talk to for the whole day so I felt a bit 'abandoned'."

My mum showed concern in her eyes.

"No Patricia today?"

She asked. I just shook my head and shrugged while curling my lip just a little.

"You will always have me and Dad Abby, you're stuck with *us*."

Her kiss on my forehead sent a warmth into me that I relished. As my parents went back to their rooms, I switched my light off and hoped for a better tomorrow, or at least one that was far less lonely than today had been.

Chapter Thirteen

Unfortunately for me the next day followed the previous one as if yesterday had never actually ended, it was exactly as awful as the day before, so much so that I settled on talking to Stinky Phil, a decision I immediately regretted when a waft of unwashed socks filled my nostrils.

"Hey Phil, what are you up to today?"

Phil peered up at me with a gormless expression.

"You know, same as everyday."

He replied. I sat on the seat adjacent to him so as to avoid being upwind of his stench.

"What game are you playing today?"

The instant I said those words I knew I would live to regret it.

Without even lifting his head he announced the title of this boring game where you get to train ninjas until they are ready to fight each other. The conversation continued to bore me to death as he went on to tell me all about his favourite ninja characters and the skills he had trained them to have, he even went on to tell me who was his best fighter including the reasons as to why that was (**UGH**). I did think to ask why his favourite ninja wasn't his best fighter however I wasn't ready to open myself up to more punishment just to find out why.

Thankfully, Phil did not have any subjects at school with me which would hopefully mean no more Phil, today at least, I eagerly rushed off into class as soon as we got to school (on time for once). Mr. Rat dropped a surprise quiz into our laps first thing in the morning, as if it was designed just to punish us or perhaps just me directly; he loved having surprise tests exactly when you wanted them the least.

I was heavily distracted by other things during the exam so much so that I wasn't even aware of what I was writing on the page half of the time, it showed because at the end of the day I was handed a test paper marked with the letter C in bold red pen.

Mr. Rat was very unhappy with me which led to an after-school detention to redo the questions all over again, despite my protests of outrage he would not budge on his decision. After being held against my will, instead of listening to the rodent *moan* and *complain*, I stared at my phone while I made noises which would allow him to think I was actually listening to his drivel.

No new messages, I opened up the texts that I had sent which read as follows:

ME: didn't C U online last night?

ME: hope UR OK?

ME: Long time no speak bestie what's good?

ME: C U online 2night? Got UR notes!

Delivered

Mr. Rat grabbed the phone out of my hand, my lack of enthusiasm was probably what was failing to impress him.

"Abigail are you even listening to me?"

I stared blankly, I had not been listening but I had heard my graded mark.

With attitude I brushed off his complaints.

"I passed this time, didn't I? You said I got an A just now."

His ratty face boiled.

"The fact you got a C this morning showed me you weren't trying at all before, furthermore your complete dismissal of it got you a detention, you seem more concerned with your social life than you are with your grades!"

I did not have time for this.

"Look, plenty of people in class get a C grade on a regular basis. It's a little unfair that I was given detention, just because I usually get A's."

I replied hastily. If looks could kill I'm pretty sure I'd be dead.

My mind was on the Patricia situation.

"I'm terribly sorry that I expect the best from my top student!"

Sarcasm dripped from his thin pursed lips.

"If you would like to end up in a dead end job, despite being fully capable of becoming something important in life, please carry on! However, if you actually want to accomplish something in life I suggest you heed my warning."

The beastly teacher had successfully got my attention.

"Next time I expect to see your best effort every time; not just when you feel like it! Or instead of a detention I will be sure to invite your parents in to discuss your drop in grades. Do I make myself clear?"

He was not playing around.

I did *not* need another lecture from that scrawny little man who would be confused for a creature that lived in the sewers about not meeting my full potential. Not with such little class time left, knowing my luck he'd find a way to get me to study in school instead of home leading up to the exams.

"OK Mr. Ra... I mean Mr. Richardson I will focus next time I promise."

The Rodent's eyes turned into barely opened slits.

"You better Miss. Wilson as next time it will be for real, no more practices left for you to half-ass."

I held my hand out to receive my phone back from the seething Mr. Richardson, I tended to have that effect on the man. I could have sworn his nose even twitched like an angry sewer rat.

Now that I was in possession of my phone again I could check if I had a reply to my messages, I did not, much to my dismay. Feeling defeated, I headed off to the late coach bus that was normally only for delinquents, slackers and sometimes it was also boarded by people attending after-school clubs in order to get home; to my utter displeasure Phil was on that very bus.

"Hey Abigail, do you want to sit next to me?"

He asked joyfully. I smiled a completely false smile as I sat in the space next to him. The smell was worse than this morning, moreover I was unfortunate to be downwind of it this time; the offensive elements of sweat and unwashed socks forced their way into my breathing apparatus; making it apparent as to why he was sitting alone in the first place.

He continued exactly where he had left off with the 'ninja game' conversation, I had the displeasure of being involved in the first time, let alone having to endure another round of it. I now knew the answer to why his favourite character was different to his strongest fighter but now I wish I didn't.

I was very thankful when my stop had finally come to save me from complete boredom, not to mention that it would stop me from passing out due to the lack of clean air I was being subjected to.

"That sounds amazing Phil you will have to finish that thought next time ok... Buh bye now..."

He briefly nodded in my direction as I exited swiftly and headed home.

Pretty sure it didn't matter who was sitting next to him, he would pretty much have the same conversation with anyone who gave him the time of day. I escaped the bus moments before my mind had officially become numb from unimportant information overload. I was still worried about Patricia so my mind wandered back over to that issue. I had been distracted by my own thoughts, so much so that I didn't notice the figure close to my residence until I nearly reached my door.

Chapter Fourteen

I had virtually given up on all hopes of hearing from my supposed friend when I started to recognise a familiarity to the figure outside of my front door waiting for me.

"Hi bestie!"

Patricia could be seen grinning from ear to ear looking very tanned, as I reached my porch I noticed a certain glow about her which only succeeded in frustrating me more.

"Hi Patricia, did your phone die?"

Patricia laughed as she waved her hand back and forth in front of my face, she was completely ignoring my scowl.

"Not here big Gail, let's go inside so I can catch you up on everything."

Intrigued as I was, I also felt a little miffed as to why I had been ignored.

I rolled my eyes as I opened the door and made sure she saw me do it.

"Come on then, this better be good"

I led our way into the lounge, nobody was home yet which meant we could have some privacy. Patricia practically sat down on top of me when cozying up next to me, she seemed as if she was going to burst.

"I have just come from Paris, Tyler whisked me away on a surprise trip, it was *so* romantic."

She announced. Patricia looked as if she had just given me an amazing gift, she seemed to be awaiting an equal response to her news. I paused slightly as her hands clung tightly to my forearm.

"How on earth could Tyler take you anywhere? Did you somehow get fake ID. You can't even book a flight without a credit card!"

I asked, fairly aggressively. Patricia was taken a back at my disbelief over her story, to be fair she often embellished in her stories but I'd let her think I believed her usually.

"So our parents were there too, you happy? Way to ruin my story… God."

Patricia complained. Her annoyance was only serving to raise the heat of my temper.

"So… you went away with your parents… What's with all the secrets then, you couldn't just tell me that when I text?"

I asked, removing my arm from her grasp.

Patricia continued, feeling a little deflated.

"Well… yeah but it was still romantic. You're just jealous. I couldn't tell you, I can't leave evidence to prove I was bunking off school, now could I? Or do you want to get my parents in trouble?"

Patricia asked. My facial expressions became perplexed.

"Why would you think I would let that happen, don't you trust me?"

I asked angrily. Patricia threw her head back in extravagant laughter.

"No, Silly, but someone could have read your message or something. We can't take any chances now, can we?"

She carried on with her story before I could even utter a sound.

Her happiness was starting to irk me.

"So anyway my lovely Tyler told me for the first time that he loved me while we were on top of the Eiffel Tower..."

I abruptly interrupted her mid-sentence.

"Patricia I get it, Tyler is a *gem,* but can we please just talk about how you didn't trust me enough to share this with me, you share everything with me; too much even if you ask me..."

Patricia's face became stern.

I felt a little nervous due to her expression.

"I didn't ask you Gail, frankly I thought you would be far happier for me than this, you don't exactly get much other excitement happening in your *own* life."

I was stunned into silence because I literally didn't have the words to express how she had just made me feel, Patricia had never been that blunt before, she didn't even use her nickname for me, which was unusual, to say the least.

I can't remember a time she ever called me anything other than 'big Gail', I know this because I secretly hated the name.

"Clearly you have no interest in hearing about Paris Gail, give me the notes you took for me so that I can go home"

I thought for a minute before I replied.

"I must have left them in my locker at school Patricia so I guess you can have them tomorrow, you will be in school tomorrow won't you? Or do you have another trip planned that I don't know about?"

Judging by her response my snide reply must have tipped her over the edge.

She was seething.

"Oh so I'm supposed to run my every decision by you am I? What are you my *mother*!?"

Her fury just inspired me to become angrier, this girl that I have known all my life, the girl who had shared everything with me has now decided that I am no longer trustworthy enough with her secrets; how am I the villain? Besides she hadn't even considered what I was currently dealing with or asked me how I was doing.

"Well I thought I was your best friend but apparently I'm just your doormat"

I replied. Patricia rose up from her seat as if to put me in my place.

She positioned her miniature hands firmly on her tiny hips, however before she could say a word I rose to my feet. She was now looking up at me as I towered over her which defeated her attempt at trying to be the bigger person.

"AARGHH!!"

She shouted at me as she began to storm off.

"AARGHH!!"

I mimicked her as she left my house in a blaze of outrage and annoyance.

"You have no right being this way with me after all I do for you!"

Patricia said. She was gone before I could think of anything to say back. Something about how she said it made me think I was missing something, I just couldn't figure out what.

Chapter Fifteen

By the time the next morning had arrived, the thought of a bus ride with Patricia, Tyler and Phil made me cringe. I felt bad for yesterday even though I didn't personally think that I had done anything wrong; except potentially making things ten times worse than I needed to.

I had sent five apology messages to her phone but there was no reply, aside from a peevish poop emoticon, which I didn't count as an actual reply. I could only assume that it meant she was unhappy with me still. I had never seen her this mad at me before, perhaps I had been taking out my frustrations out on her.

I knew I would have to admit defeat in order to get my friend back, Patricia was a lot of things but being forgiving wasn't one of them. I saw her sitting next to Tyler on the bus, as always, I was determined to be courageous as I sat in the seat behind them. It was either that or continue a very much unwanted conversation with the dreaded Phil, anything was better than that.

"Hi Patricia, hey Tyler… How are *things*?"

Tyler turned around intending to speak to me until Patricia yanked on his sleeve which led him to sink back into his seat like the coward he was.

I added a little desperation into my voice for effect.

"Patricia, I said 'I'm sorry' isn't that enough? I'm not even wrong and yet I *still* apologised!"

Patricia turned around as quick as a flash.

"*Not* wrong!? I know you had those notes on you last night so you can add being a liar to your list of crimes!"

She was right, I did have the notes and I even did her homework out of guilt over lying. I didn't want to give it to her until she agreed to forgive me. I decided to bribe her in order to gain her forgiveness, it was all I had left up my sleeves.

I opened my bag and pulled out her most favourite thing in the world; a white chocolate cheesecake. I had begged my mum to make it for me last night just in case I needed it.

"Oh Patricia, if you don't want to forgive me, who will eat all of this *delicious* white chocolate cheesecake that I happen to have with me?"

Patricia glanced at the yummy dessert using the corner of her eye, then she let out the loudest scoffing noise. Tyler seemed overly eager to accept the dessert on her behalf but my angry scowl sent his smile away.

Glancing back at my peace offering she sighed softly.

"Fine! You have my forgiveness but only because you cheated big Gail, you know I can't resist your mum's snowy delight pudding."

This was the name she had chosen to call it some years ago, I grabbed her from behind to give her a quick squeeze. I strangely enjoyed hearing that awful nickname once again.

"Thanks Patz."

She shrugged in response.

"Yeah, Yeah. You're welcome!"

Tyler relaxed his body, finally, as we both smiled at each other.

His awkward smile returned.

"Happy to see you two friends again."

He was clearly worried we would start another row again.

I felt as if I was on the losing side of that argument but it was Patricia after all so I wasn't going to win, she knew I couldn't stand her being mad at me; she was my only friend after all. I passed her the notes that I had taken for her in class alongside her completed homework then continued the bus ride with my headphones in; my favourite song played and things were back to how they should be at least.

I could have been annoyed over the fact that she neither acknowledged nor thanked me for actually doing her homework for her, just as I could have complained about her not sharing the cheesecake slice with me. I most definitely should have spoken up when she left half for Tyler who binned a good chunk of it. It just isn't in my nature to say what's on my mind, I hated confrontation and could only ever say what was on my mind when emotionally charged.

The last few days of school left much to be desired, it was exam central in the Hall which meant no time for socialising. I managed to complete a decent study session on Sunday over the weekend, I also would get my parents to pop quiz me the night before each day of the exams so that I would be as prepared as I could be.

The Hall became a room full of frustration and stress, students from the popular crews to people like me all joining together in the same fate, from Jock to Cheerleader to nerd we all had to endure the pressure of letting thirty questions on a page determine how smart we really were.

Even though I had begun to feel the heat by the time Friday came along, we were sent home with these very serious looking envelopes; they had our results inside of them. I was waiting until I got home so that I could open it with my parents, I couldn't wait to see their faces; so long as I passed them.

One good thing about all of this studying and exam sitting was that it distracted me from my Patricia drama. Despite saying she forgave me she had been indifferent towards me, a fact I chose to ignore for my own sanity. I'd much rather pretend all was okay in the world than admit I was alone in it.

Patricia and Tyler said their farewells at the school due to the lift home they were getting without me. I had tried to ask if I could join them when she first started receiving lifts. Her excuses became thinner and thinner until I just gave up asking. I would watch on enviously as I saw them get into a car that clearly had space for me and drive away.

So, I rode the bus just as I had too many times before. I had been so distracted by the day's events to notice the obscure welcoming party at my front door.

This time, however, it was my parents who could be seen out on the porch; they were waiting with a big balloon that had Congratulations written on it. The writing was so large that it could have seen from yards away if I had been paying attention.

"You don't know what my results are yet."

I shouted in their direction as I grew nearer to the house. By the time I had reached them my parents engulfed me in a three-way embrace.

"It doesn't matter to us Abby, we are just as proud of a C as we are of an A"

My dad always knew just what to say in these situations.

"Just so long as you did your best"

Mum hastily added.

She sounded a bit like Mr Rat, I perish the thought of coming home with a D. I wouldn't want to cause heart failure for my old nemesis nor would I for my parents. It's unthinkable for me to receive anything less than an A grade.

For once, I would love to be one of those regular people who were proud of their B,C or even D grade. But no, I had to be one of those smart perfectionist types who would never live anything other than an A down. With that thought in mind I was terrified of what the paperwork in my hand might read. What if I choked on them all?

I started opening the envelope with expectation filling my mind. I shuddered with excitement and fear.

"Don't hold us in suspense, Abby"

My mother practically snatched the envelope out of my hands.

"Let me see too, wow all A's well-done girl, never had a doubt."

Dad stood proudly before me.

"Well done Abby, now let's go inside and eat your congratulations cake."

Mum ushered us all into the house and cut us a slice each of this oversized red velvet cake which was covered in creamy frosting.

"Thanks guys, you're the best."

I stuffed my face full of yummy cake whilst nearly forgetting that tomorrow was our last day here in Atlanta before travelling to England for three months.

No amount of cake was going to make that information digest any better. Seven in the evening had arrived, so I rushed to my computer in order to talk with Patricia. As predicted **PATZIE<3 TYLER 4va** was appearing online with a joyous green dot next to it. Our conversations went as follows:

Gail :¬P

Hey Patz! What grades did u get!?

PATZIE<3 TYLER 4va

U know, just an A, 2 B's and C :¬D!

Gail :¬P

Well done! I'm so happy 4 U!

PATZIE<3 TYLER 4va

How bout U big Gail?

Gail :¬P

All A's

PATZIE<3 TYLER 4va

Surprise, Surprise

Gail :¬P

C U tomoz?

PATZIE<3 TYLER 4va

C u tomoz

She logged off straight away after that, our last chance to see each other before I left was tomorrow so I hoped to see her alone; an unlikely but not impossible option.

We hadn't spoken much over the last few days of school due to our exams being at different times and the lifts she was getting from Tyler's parents. Tomorrow was going to be such good fun, it might be the last dose of fun for quite some time.

Chapter Sixteen

School was finally over which normally would have brought me such joy, however with the impending travel plans to visit England looming ever closer the only feeling I could conjure up was desperation. My mum had booked the flights which meant we were leaving first thing in the morning, the only good thing about today is that my mum had invited all our friends over for a BBQ to say goodbye. This was our last chance to see everyone before we disappeared for three months. I was dressed in my 'Sunday best', a saying my mum used any time I made an effort with my appearance (which, to be fair, was hardly ever).

I was dubious about my outfit choice at first, last year my mum had bought this dress for me yet I hadn't worn it yet. It didn't fit me properly until now due to the fact that I couldn't provide enough cleavage for it back then. The dress looked much better with more curves rather than less.

With help I managed to make myself unrecognisable using my mum's makeup stash. She hardly ever let me use it, clearly her guilt over ruining my summer had started to take effect. The reflection looking back at me was this unfamiliar girl, I could have passed for one of those popular girls at school.

After I straightened my hair it flowed down past my waist, the stranger staring back at me caused me to pause. I considered wiping the makeup off of my face and shoving my hair back up into a squishy bun, after taking in a deep breathe I forced those feelings deep down inside of me. I wanted to make a special effort for the occasion. I had been out of sorts lately, I had always felt a bit like an outsider to my own life but recent events had escalated this fact. I was never one to make a fuss, there was never a right time to tell people you felt alone even when in a sea of people.

Not many would understand that statement, I much preferred to play the role of a happy go lucky jokester than to get real about my feelings. I was excited to show off my new look to Patricia, unfortunately for me she was running late and hadn't arrived yet.

I was assigned to babysitting duty, for the neighbours kids (they were on Santa's naughty list for sure) so I could definitely use some company. So long as she turned up before the tiny terrors managed to ruin my look I could cope with the little brats.

Mum had me hide all the good ornaments so they couldn't break any of them, we learned the hard way last time we had a get together. All of our friends and neighbours were there which included the terrible threesome. They managed to break this crystal swan that my dad had bought for my mum on their tenth wedding anniversary. It was worth a lot of money, or so my mum thought, in fact Dad and I had found it at a yard sale for only a dollar fifty.

She became extremely distraught over losing her 'expensive' gift. We could have easily let the little demons spawn off the hook by revealing the real price. Dad didn't have the heart to tell her the truth so she still goes on about her pricey swan being brutally murdered by the neighbours' kids; they deserve my mum's wrath so I feel no sympathy towards the evil gremlins. As soon as Patricia got here I could sneak off to my room and avoid the party all together, she was (as per usual) taking her sweet time to get here.

As I had predicted the Moore family arrived in style, they rocked up outside of our formidable home exiting a raven coloured convertible. It looked as though Patricia and her parents were floating across the lawn, they glided so gracefully towards us. I burst through the front door to greet them.

"Hey Patz, what took you so long? I got stuck with those out of control children again!"

Patricia seemed a little embarrassed by my display.

Forcing a grin on her face to try to steer me away from her parents

"Okay Abigail, let's go back inside shall we?"

She shoved me forward into my living room that had now been transformed into party central.

"Nice to see you again Mr. and Mrs. Moore."

They had followed us in so I waved at them (a bit too enthusiastically). Patricia's parents always made me feel a little on edge as if I wouldn't be allowed to sneeze without first having their permission to do so.

One time when I was visiting them as a kid, we sat around their incredibly large dining table, coq au van was served which was supposed to be a French delicacy. I don't personally think it had enough flavour so I asked for Patricia to pass me the salt (it really needed it).

Their faces looked as if I had farted at the dinner table or something just as vile, such offended gazes were peering at me. With every shake of the salt onto my plate I lost an inch of my size until I felt only two feet tall in their gigantic chairs, how Patricia was even able to get into the chairs is beyond me. She could have easily been confused for a small toddler sitting in them.

I wasn't invited around for dinner much after that.

"Hello Abigail, where are your parents? We have a gift for them."

Patricia's mum faced me with a stern expression causing me to gulp

"Outside with the BBQ, Mrs. Moore."

I grinned awkwardly as they hurried outside. Patricia started laughing at me.

"Oh big Gail, you crack me up, they still haven't forgiven you for insulting our chef's food."

I blushed ever so slightly a little embarrassed.

Patricia barely even tried to hide her laughter that was at my expense, I could have asked why she hadn't laughed outside when her parents were a witness but I chose to keep quiet.

"Well clearly your chef needs to learn how to cook for us 'common folk'."

I stuck out my tongue abruptly.

"Do you know you're wearing a dress big Gail? Are you feeling well?"

I glanced down at my beautiful dress so that I could admire my look once more.

I stood by my decision; the outfit worked.

"Hey I make this look good, don't you think?"

I winked playfully.

"Well it's okay, I guess, but not very 'you' if you know what I mean."

She winked back at me as if to mock me.

"What do you mean by that? Not 'me'?"

Patricia shrugged.

"Well, you know, you're a banana split kind of girl and this outfit is more suited for a creme brûlée girl."

I was a touch offended by her comments.

She loved to throw fancy foods in my face knowing that I had never tried them before, I could ask her chef to make me a creme brûlée however he'd likely serve me a flavourless lump to eat. I used my good old fashioned sense of humour to save the day.

"I do like my banana splits."

I tried to laugh it off but it did sting a *teensy* bit. I thought she would have been happy because I had finally made an effort with my appearance, instead she had just implied that I didn't belong in the clothes that I was wearing.

Exchanging gifts was next on the agenda, seeing as the pleasantries were all over and done with. I passed my gift over into Patricia's delicate hands, I had used all my saved-up pocket money to buy her an extendable selfie stick that held her phone.

"It is to help you take 'smoochy pics' with 'perfect hair' Tyler."

I teased her as she handed me her gift. She seemed indifferent to my present; shaking off my feelings of inadequacy I focused on unwrapping my present.

She bought me a new set of headphones, they were state of the art of course.

"I thought you might like some working headphones, for a change, big Gail."

I grabbed her tightly and squeezed the life out of her.

"Thank You."

Patricia winced.

"Okay, OK! Tiny human here struggling to breathe."

I burst into laughter which promptly turned into tears.

"I'll miss you, Patz."

I dried my eyes.

"Yes well, don't get all soppy on me, it is *only* for the summer."

We reminisced over old times, good and bad, for about half an hour before going back to our parents.

Chapter Seventeen

My father was wearing his favourite apron saying 'kiss the chef' on it, while my mother just blended into the chair that she was sitting in. On the other hand you had Patricia's parents Stephen and Geraldine wearing expensive clothing and jewellery that was probably worth more than our entire house (contents and all).

I wasn't gallant enough to use their first names personally; my parents seemed at ease around them, seemingly oblivious to their class difference. Such a strange group of people surrounded me, the only thing these people had in common was that they knew my family.

The rest of the party went by quite quickly, Patricia and her parents were one of the first people to leave our little soiree. It really wasn't their scene but at least they had shown up. It was lovely to see Patricia one last time before we were reduced to pen pals for a summer. I hugged her before promising to write and keep in touch, a vow which I had every intention of sticking to. What else would I have to do in a country like England?

I could picture it now: sipping tea, discussing the weather whilst eating crumpets. A shudder ran down my spine at the thought. The worst part was that I was going to miss the party at the lake that we went to every summer holiday, there was nothing better than watching the awkward encounter between my parents and hers.

My dad would make garish jokes while my mum tried to shush him as the Moore family grin and bear him. I loved my dad even though he was embarrassing; he gave the greatest cuddles known to man which basically meant he could get away with anything.

All that was left to do was to pack my hand luggage for the flight so I headed upstairs and tried to figure out what I needed while travelling on a plane. Mum told me that riding planes were just like the school bus but high in the sky instead of on the ground. I assume instead of being stuck in traffic we may get stuck behind a flock of birds, either way headphones would be a definite requirement.

Thanks to Patricia I had fully functioning ones to pack. I viewed my room one final time, I couldn't see anything else that I needed which meant that I was officially packed and ready for my flight to England.

I started to wonder what my grandmother might look like, since they had become estranged she didn't have any pictures of her to show me. I thought maybe I would get to speak with her over the phone but my mother said it was for the best if we spoke in person for the first time, maybe she wanted to make sure I didn't upset her with any of my awkward jokes that I enjoyed making. I asked her if I would be getting backdated presents for all the birthdays and Christmases she missed but her steely glare told me that wasn't going to be happening somehow.

I always wondered what having a grandparent was like so at least I was going to find out soon enough. I was under strict instructions to speak correctly wherever possible and to try not to offend her. I could only be me, was I going to offend her by being me? Well yes, I have upset people by accident many times so that probably wouldn't be a very hard task for me to accomplish.

Going back some time now, there was an incident with Mr. Rat during a Math's lesson, I had gotten stuck on a question as it had been written down incorrectly. I made the fatal mistake of pointing out, in front of the class, his error; upon recognising it for himself a mortified expression took over his face.

I realised that I should have quite possibly kept my foot out of my mouth on that one, he wasn't keen on me after that, he always called me by my full name and tried so very hard to catch me out on any mistakes I happened to make; that way he could parade them around for the whole class to see. I had originally thought I was being helpful, pointing out his spelling mistakes in the question, we clearly did not see eye to eye on this issue.

The morning of our flight I was woken up at an inhumane hour of the morning, the sun hadn't even woken up yet, why should I be out of my comfy bed? Mum had to take the duvet away from me before I was willing to accept my fate. With the cold of the morning attacking every fibre of my being, I had no choice but to drag myself into an upright position. I turned on the shower to full pelt and scraped off my PJs ready to jump into the inviting warm water.

I needed a wakeup call or I wasn't going to make it into the car. The water on my face was exhilarating, the sheer force of the water helped my brain to catch up with my body and join me in the real world. I got dressed, grabbed my bag and headed down to our neighbours' little, old car ready for my first experience in flying; I was even starting to look forward to seeing this so-called 'England'.

Firstly, we had to endure a car journey to the airport driven by our creepy neighbour Milo; he was very friendly but extremely abnormal. The man was balding on the top of his head with only the sides of his head covered in any sort of hair, on the other hand his beard was full and lustrous. He loved singing loudly to the point that even your own thoughts could not be heard. I know this from experience

The worst part was that his clothes were probably fashionable twenty years ago which more than likely was when he bought them (judging by their faded appearance).

His beard was bright ginger with shades of white all the way through it while his hair on his head, at least what remained on his head, was completely colourless without a single ginger hair in sight. Spitballs flew out of his nearly toothless mouth when he spoke to you, always with such excitement in the tone of his voice about the simplest of things.

He once found a quarter on the ground, however the way he told the story, you would have thought he found the mythical pot of gold at the end of the rainbow. It was his eyes that creeped me out the most, they were the colour of titanium and only one was real, the other was a glass eye that the Doctors had given him after he had to have one removed. The story of why he lost it and how he came to have a glass one differed every time he told it, he loved to tell tall tales as much as we loved to listen to them.

My favourite version of the story was the one where a savage dog had ripped out his eyeball leaving him eyeless on one side. Milo was an extremely fast driver so we arrived at the airport in no time at all, unsurprisingly, his aged car appeared to be barely functioning on the outside but inside was pure horsepower.

He helped us unpack our luggage from his boot then he got back on his way home, my parents thanked him profusely for taking us so early in the morning, he welcomed the thanks gladly as he got in his way.

The airport was so very large and full of people differing in sizes and ages, humans from all different walks of life all coming together for one purpose; to fly on a plane. After checking in, we then had to wait for a very long time just to be able to board this thing that had the appearance of a glorified tin can with wings; such chaos surrounding us.

There were some people checking the time while others were making sure they had their passports still in their possessions, finally the rest were huffing and puffing about the uncomfortable chairs and delayed flights.

My mum and dad were just as bad, messing around checking inside their bags every five minutes just to make sure their passports hadn't got up and wandered away somehow, they had their bags pinned to their chests (I highly doubt anyone could steal them away). I hadn't been allowed to hold onto anything of worth such as a passport or boarding pass. Me, the lowly child, could never be trusted with such a difficult task.

I had come to the conclusion there was no better time than now to give Patricia an update before I was forced to place my phone on the dreaded 'aeroplane mode' (Ugh, perish the thought), no internet access meant I could do next to nothing on my phone, thankfully I had downloaded all of my favourite tunes onto my mp3 player so that I could listen to them whilst in the skies. My text session didn't last as long as I thought it was going to as you can see:

ME: In the airport waiting 2 board the aeroplane!

PATRICIA: Boring! Message me when U get there!

ME: OK Patz! TY again 4 the headphones

Delivered

Apparently, my phone wouldn't work over in England properly because of the network system being different, my mother promised me that she would sort it out as soon as we landed; a promise I would try and make sure that she kept.

On the plane, it was far quieter than the waiting room, once everyone had found their assigned seats they all cozied in and relaxed ready to take off; I loved the air hostess ladies going up and down with their carts. They all looked so beautiful with their matching lipstick and neck scarves tied into a perfect knot; so smiley and polite. Despite the exorbitant prices of the items that they were selling, the stewardesses still managed to sell a lot. This was probably due to their appearance more than the quality of the items being sold.

Dad bought the nuts while my mum went for the white wine spritzer, I got crisps and an in-flight movie for us all to enjoy. After the film was over, we all drifted off to sleep. I began dreaming of me being an English lady in a British romance novel, I was looking forward to a whole new set of books to get into, this time with English heroines to read about instead. In just six hours we would land in London and a new adventure awaited us, I had no idea what to expect, which was terrifying yet also exciting.

Chapter Eighteen

England at last! Getting off the plane was very stiff as we queued up to exit the confinements we had all been squeezed into, the air had become stale from all the recycled breath. The impatient passengers had been sat, breathing that same oxygen in and out for more than eight hours straight, forced to share an environment with strangers in cramped seating.

When we finally managed to gather our belongings, we headed out of the plane in order to get our suitcases from the ever-turning conveyor belt of bags. There was a man in a penguin suit holding up the name Wilson on a plaque.

"Mum, Dad, why does Grandma Jean look as if she is dressed like a male butler?"

They both turned around as if in a daze unamused by my attempt at wit.

"That is possibly because that is one of Grandma Jean's' many chauffeurs, dear, not Grandma Jean."

My mother replied to my question while my dad still looked as if he didn't even know his own name, let alone who the man with the sign was.

"Um... okay... but why a chauffeur?"

My dad drifted back into reality as he woke up from his daydream; finally.

While huddling all our luggage he replied to my question.

"That is because Grandma Jean is filthy rich, Hun."

A look of bafflement covered my face. All of my life we have lived a life of mediocrity only to find out that our life could have been first class instead. I tried to fathom the concept but it was lost on me. We followed the strange man to a stretch limousine, it was so shiny that I could brush my teeth while using it as a mirror.

The interior was even fancier than the exterior with cream leather seats and a roof that opened. Shiny, gold trimmings were everywhere you laid your eyes. The seats were so comfortable that you couldn't even recognise the fact that you were indeed sitting down, classical music played from the arm rests where tiny speakers were hidden inside of them. I felt as though I could live in this thing that my relative used to transport people in.

As we were arriving in the grounds of Grandma Jean's Mansion I drew the window down so I could observe it all first hand, the gate opened as we pulled up as if by magic, like it knew we had arrived. It was so grand but very slow moving; it towered above us while it ebbed inch by inch until there was room enough for us to pass through. The driveway was nearly as long as a runway at the airport, with beautiful fountains shooting water high into the sky surrounded by gloriously green grass.

There was an array of flowers in every colour of the rainbow which lined the pathway up to the entrance of this glorious building. There was a real live butler waiting for us and he helped us with our luggage which now looked so out of place amongst the possessions of this wealthy woman, to my right stood yet another member of my grandma's staff who announced her entering as she came in to greet us.

Who was this woman with such extravagant taste, how is it that I was raised in a dump while my blood relative lived like a queen? This elderly, regal looking lady came to the top of the stairs holding tightly to a cane, with the help of her staff she sat in the stair lift that had been affixed to the railing. I tried hard not to stare but my mouth remained agape the whole time she was travelling down her grand staircase.

Such a modern feature in a traditional house seemed to be a bit miss-matched however seeing as she had only a few months to live it was probably very much needed. It did look brand new as if it had hardly been used, I wasn't sure if they bought a new one each morning or was just very well looked after. Her cane was a unique looking thing, there was a 'W' hand carved into the top of it with gold sealing off the ends, an echoing click could be heard each time she tapped it along the ground as she walked.

My grandmother stepped down off of the stairlift and gracefully stood before us.

"Hi Mum, this is Abigail our daughter, it is so nice to see you again..."

My mother was soon silenced by hers.

"Deidre we need no introduction but thank you for the unneeded commentary, now Abigail let me take a look at you, *finally*."

She scanned me up and down then moved my face side to side, she even made me bare my teeth as if she was checking for cavities.

I tried to break the tense silence.

"Um... Hi?"

I waved a short, small wave as I felt very much like a square peg being rammed into a circle shaped hole. Grandma Jean turned from me back to my mother again.

"I suppose you didn't do a terrible job of raising the girl, she does seem to be healthy enough, now go with Henry and get settled in the guest bedrooms as I tell the chef to prepare for our evening meal."

She gestured to the butler and we followed along behind him as per her instructions.

The meet and greet didn't happen as I had imagined it would, I figured there would be tears and hugs flying around the place but instead I got a room full of tension you could only cut through if you were using a chainsaw.

Our rooms were as impressive as the rest of the house, we each had our own bathroom, bedroom and our very own man servant; mine was called Cliff as I found out by reading his badge. I had no real experience with people waiting on me but I did feel a little unnerved in his presence.

Cliff was extremely helpful, despite my objections he had unpacked for me each and every item without even so much as a rosy cheek in site; he was a man of few words, very proper and dignified. To be honest I couldn't get a word out of him but I assume he spoke.

I did however wonder why my mother and father had been separated into two different rooms, maybe Grandma Jean was opposed to them sharing as she was against their union in the first place. Cliff was not willing to answer the smallest of queries so I didn't bother asking him why.

Chapter Nineteen

My phone was not working yet as my mum didn't stick to her end of the bargain that we had made. She didn't seem in control of anything we were doing since her mum had made contact. I did have my laptop, which Cliff had kindly set up for me, as efficient as he was I preferred to do things for myself. I checked the time but it wasn't seven in Atlanta yet so I decided to wait until after dinner to try and catch Patricia; if I could stay awake that long.

There was a knock at my bedroom door.

"Come in Cliff, don't worry... I'm decent."

The door creaked open as I glanced over towards the direction of the noise, I noticed a figure very unlike Cliff entering the room.

"My dear, sorry to disturb you, but I felt we needed some time to 'catch up' seeing as we have never met before today."

It was the dreaded Grandma Jean, not Cliff, as I had first presumed.

"Oh... um... Hello there."

I frantically jumped down from the bed and tried to adjust my appearance to look a little less disheveled.

"Calm down."

Her expression softened.

"*Abby,* is it? Or do you prefer Abigail'?"

Her persona seemed to have changed since our meeting earlier.

She was less grizzly than before.

"Well I get called all sorts so I don't mind, shall I call you Grandma?"

Her laugh echoed in the lofty room.

"All sorts? One should only ever be called by their given name. Jean will do fine, Abby dear. I have never been, nor do I hope to ever be called 'grandma'."

Her hand touched mine as she gestured for me to sit next to her on the bed.

"You don't like being called 'Grandma'?"

She paused for a moment before answering me.

I had thought it to be a simple yes or no question.

"Well, you see, I haven't exactly been a part of your life, much to my dismay; my dear girl. I fear Grandma is too formal, It wouldn't be fair on you, to expect for you to call me family until it felt right. When you're ready, you can call me whatever it is that feels appropriate to you. I'm sure I can 'adjust'."

I was taken aback by her thoughtfulness.

The stories I heard about her were of this fierce woman who cared only for herself.

"Okay *Jean*, so why have I never met you before now? Or even know about you for that matter?"

I raised my eyebrows expectantly.

"If I had my way that would *never* have happened. I couldn't control your mother, she was so determined to disgrace our family name, I had to force her to keep you; despite how you came to be."

I removed my hand from hers.

I folded my arms a little uncomfortable at what she was insinuating.

"What do you mean you *forced* her to keep me? She ran away so she could have me, *you* tried to steal me from her and raise me as your own... right?"

My lip quivered as she shook her head slowly.

"There are two sides to every story Abigail. Your mother clearly didn't want you to know, I'm sorry, I thought they had told you the full truth."

She paused for dramatic effect despite clearly having more to say.

I didn't want to believe what she was saying.

"You are a growing woman Abigail and if you would like me to tell you what *really* happened, I can... but it will not be easy for you to hear."

My arms felt limp as I tried to decide if I should kick her out of my room or beg for her to spill all the details.

"I...I... I don't know."

Tears fell from my eyes uncontrollably.

I had tried to be positive about what was happening but there was no humour to be found in this situation.

"Come here, my sweet child."

I had never cried in front of anyone apart from my parents before. I was completely out of my depth, I felt like screaming but all that came out of my mouth were these pathetic whimpers. I wanted to stand up tall and tell her to get her lying butt out of my room but I couldn't be certain that her words were lies. Truthfully I had no idea what other secrets had been kept from me, I spent my life believing one thing only to find out I was wrong.

Grandma Jean decided to pull me into her chest and rub my back as if I was only five years old, I felt as if I were only five years old at that moment so I just let her do it.

"Your mother tried to hide you from me, she went to the clinic with your Uncle and planned for an abortion, thankfully a friend spotted her and called me immediately."

Every word hit me like a dagger to my chest, I didn't know how much more I could take.

I wanted to run away but I had nowhere to go.

"After I forced her to keep the child she grew attached to you and resolved to run away. She was too stubborn to accept my help in raising you. So she fled to America, as I have recently discovered. I tried all this time to find you and finally managed to... just in time I hope."

I sat up and rubbed away the tears in my eyes, my sorrow had been replaced with fury.

"Why would my parents lie to me?"

I was distraught.

Just then there was another knock on the door, this time it really was Cliff, he was summoning us to dinner.

"Thank you Cliff, we will be right there."

She turned her attention back onto me again.

"Now Abby, straighten up. It's time to eat, you will have time to discuss this further with me later, if that is what you desire."

Just like that our conversation was over. She disappeared out of my room as quickly as she had entered.

Left to my own devices I tried to make sense of what had just been said to me, however all I got for my efforts was a dull ache in my head. I was left with more questions than I had arrived with, instead of my original question being answered they had now just been multiplied instead. Who was this Uncle that I had never heard of before? (yet more family I probably had to endure) I scraped my feet along the floor trying to resist the dreadful dinner that awaited me.

Chapter Twenty

Grandma Jean sat at the head of the table with my parents either side of her, the table seemed to go on for miles. I passed so many empty chairs on the way to my seat, I couldn't help but wonder if she spent most nights alone at this very table.

Seven plates were laid out which led me to believe that company was expected. I couldn't fathom who might be joining us, this mysterious Uncle and his family maybe, I just knew I didn't want to be there.

My mum and dad had forced grins on their faces as they opened my chair up for me to sit with them.

"Who's joining us?"

I asked. Grandma Jean decided to be the one to answer.

"Observant as ever Abigail. Your Aunt, my other daughter Christina and her family will be joining us. They have been looking forward to meeting you."

As she finished her sentence Cliff announced the presence of the Robinson family, they were standing together; a man, a woman and a girl about my age.

The man was tall and very slim while the lady was nearly identical to my mum, all apart from her long blonde hair draping past her shoulders. She was dressed in an extremely posh frock, she looked very upper class unlike my mother.

My mum had her mousy brown hair pulled back as usual on the other hand Aunty Christina's hair was straight and flowed down her back; so glossy. I was slightly envious of my aunt's look, I'm sure if my mum made more of an effort over her appearance she could look just as elegant.

Their daughter was short whilst having a plump figure but she had her mum's face, she was pretty but hid it well with large glasses and acne covering her whole face which led me to believe that she may be in fact younger than me. William leapt up to his feet and greeted them all.

"Christina, Jeremy, I can't believe you guys got married. Who's this little angel you have here?"

He embraced them all one by one.

"This is Juliette, long time no see *bro*, you packed on a few pounds since we last spoke."

Jeremy stayed silent allowing Christina to answer for him. There was a certain look she gave him that had me thinking there may be some bad blood between them.

My dad looked as if he had seen a ghost, he quickly turned back to sit in his chair. It was almost as though he'd been caught up in the nostalgia of seeing old friends that he had forgotten all about some deep dark secret that now loomed over his head again. Why was she calling him 'bro' in that tone of voice? She was clearly very unhappy about something.

"Hi *sis*, it is so nice to have all the family here under one roof."

Christina stared at my mum while she was just looking down at her empty plate, Christina didn't seem all that pleased to see her sister again. I watched the awkwardness simmer until Aunty Christina turned her gaze onto me next.

"Go sit down Juliette, opposite your cousin Abigail."

They all took their places at the table. Before long the food had arrived, silence had infected us, all you could hear was the sound of soup being poured into bowls and placed on top of our plates.

I have to admit the soup was top class but eating it was not worth the tension that surrounded us.

"Let's say Grace first, please."

I peered up from my bowl with the spoon still inside my mouth and quickly placed it back onto the table. I bared my teeth in an attempt to smile, Grandma Jean didn't look very pleased with me nor with my parents at my lack of dinner etiquette.

"We thank God for our food before we eat it in *this* residence Abigail."

I wanted to say something quippy but decided against it.

I had literally no idea that I came from a family who said 'Grace' before we ate, the most we did back in America was mutter thanks to the chef of the day. Her steely gaze fell upon my parents as they sheepishly hid their faces.

"How about you do the honours Abigail, I'm sure your mother has taught you how."

Jean added. She hadn't but I wasn't about to rat her out. I only knew of one prayer so I began despite my hesitancy.

"Our father who art in heaven…"

Grandma Jean cut me off.

"We aren't in church Abigail, just say something simple and from the heart."

She said. I thought back to a book I once read about a religious family, I went with something simple.

"Thank you Lord for blessing us with this food, we pray for all of our family to be safe and well. Amen."

As I had started the prayer everyone bowed their heads and closed their eyes so I did too.

I believe I passed her test considering I had no complaints after it was all over. I quietly finished my soup having lost the will to make any sort of humour of this situation. Juliette was also very silent as she twisted her spoon around inside her bowl.

"Not a fan of soup, I take it."

She shrugged.

"I'll eat yours if you like."

Juliette smiled coyly. The adults were busy passing pleasantries over the dinner table so I did a quick switcheroo of the bowls. Juliette happily pretended to have eaten her food whilst I helped myself to a second bowl.

The dinner was just awful (despite the delicious food), no one had even noticed that I was upset. The fact that I had complete strangers surrounding me whilst peering into my empty soup bowl didn't help my mood. I gazed deep into my bowl as if instead of being cooked vegetables it was in fact an abyss of doom, I could not escape the words that I had heard less than an hour ago. No thoughts were even in my head, just a sadness that had taken over my soul like I had never experienced before, I felt nothing and with that I became nothing.

Juliette tried her best to keep me talking but I ran out of things to say pretty quickly. Her parents hadn't even bothered to try and engage in conversation with me. My parents seemed so fixated on the drama of Grandma Jean and her terminal cancer, a fact I should be gloomy about but who had the time when so much else was happening. Summer time with friends has been my one and only joy in life and I had to trade it in for an awkward dinner party with people who clearly didn't like each other.

I came to the decision that it was time that I branched out on my own, nobody understood me and I knew they never would. There was chatter of a trip to Oxford which inspired an idea to enter into my clever little mind. As soon as the opportunity comes my way, I'm going back to America... I would not be stopped! I had nothing good here. There was no way I could last the whole summer here! Patricia would put me up for a few weeks, if not I'll just hide out in my house.

My parents needed to take Grandma Jean to a hospital in Oxford for an experimental treatment for her lung cancer. It would take them a week's travel, I knew they would try to force me into coming along. I'm sure I can come up with a good excuse to be left behind. I would have to come up with one fast as they were leaving the day after tomorrow. I no longer wanted to know my family's sordid secrets, I just wanted to leave and get back to a place that I belonged; a place where I had a friend who understood me.

Our empty dishes were removed and replaced with some sort of meat, it appeared as if it would walk off of the plate if I let it. I was not going to eat the half alive beast leaking all over my plate. I excused myself from the table and asked to go to my room as I was feeling 'jet-lagged', I needed time to hatch my plan. I also needed some breathing space. I did my best thinking when left to my own devices. I didn't much care to be in the company of anyone in this house. Although Juliette seemed nice we were clearly worlds apart.

My mum tried to see what was wrong but Jean put an end to her questions when she hushed her and told her to leave me be. It was as though this old, rich woman had taken over the parenting part of my life; a fact which I didn't enjoy one bit. I logged online but no Patricia, it didn't matter, I would be back home soon enough enjoying our lake party together just as we did every year.

I was tired of thinking so I laid my head onto the pillow fully clothed, falling fast asleep within minutes (maybe I was a little jet-lagged after all). Tomorrow is another day, maybe when I woke up the events of the day would all just be a bad dream; not even my best fiction novel could fix this hole that I had found myself trapped inside of.

Chapter Twenty-One

I kept myself hidden in my room for most of the next day, I knew that my parents couldn't be avoided forever. They had become my enemies overnight; not that they were actually aware of this (which was exactly the way I intended on keeping it). I wanted them to remain in a false sense of security so that I could escape this prison they currently had me locked away in.

This Mansion had become my tall tower with no way out, it was being guarded by a fire breathing dragon (yes my grandma was that very dragon). I didn't know who to trust or who to turn to, strangers and liars were around every corner of this despicable dwelling of despair. The never ending hallways matched the endless feeling of loneliness I had inside.

It must have been close to two in the afternoon, England time, when Cliff stopped by to check in on me. Was it too much to ask for a simple yet polite smile? The man appeared to be emotionless, he did bring me something of use though. The mute butler had with him a simple mobile phone that was apparently a present from my grandma. She knew I hadn't gotten mine up and running yet and had used it as a way to get into my good graces. I wasn't going to be won over that easily.

It couldn't have come at a better time, I originally thought about ringing Patricia to complain about my situation however an even better idea sparked in my mind. Milo was awake at all sorts of random hours of the night and day so I knew he would answer the phone, hearing his voice was a charming reminder of home. With his help I would just need to borrow some items from my unsuspecting parents. Everything I needed for my trip to America was in my mum's room.

All I needed was a ride to the lake party (this is where Milo came in), I should make it just in time for a round of pina colada mock-tails but only if I leave first thing after my parents take Grandma Jean to Oxford. Milo seemed eager to help and agreed to meet me at the airport for the time that I was due to land. With everything in place, I decided to show my face and join everyone for dinner.

"Are you okay Abby? Darling, you look very pale."

My mum had already been sucked in by my deceit, the sympathy in my mother's eyes reassured me that she would go along with letting me stay behind tomorrow.

I of course added my best 'brave face' voice that I had before reassuring her that I was fine.

"The chef will be serving roasted tomatoes on bruschetta, pan fried quail with summer vegetables and for dessert panna cotta with a raspberry coulis."

The chef had loudly announced to the table; I had no idea what any of it meant nor did I wish to find out.

I don't know if I could get used to all of this fancy food, there were so many different courses being served. Hopefully if my arrangement works out I will be back home eating sloppy joes in no time at all, those pineapple shaped ice cubes were calling my name and I intended on answering.

I moved my food around the plate, wincing every chance I got.

"You don't seem well, perhaps you should go lie down Abby."

My mum said. I sighed loudly while walking slowly passed them. I had put my face into the steamy shower to make it sweaty before coming to the table. As I grew closer my dad looked worried.

"Oh dear, is it that time of the month again?"

Without knowing it, my dad had just given me the perfect idea. No way they could force me to travel whilst suffering with bad period pains.

I convinced them that I had severe menstrual cramps which would mean I needed to stay in bed resting.

"Mum it's really bad this time, I can barely walk..."

I screwed up my face as if I were in agony. My mother seemed annoyed.

"Okay Abby darling, if you insist, you can stay here. But you must call us if you have any problems. I don't like the thought of leaving you alone."

Mum said as she hugged me tight. I felt guilt rising up but I had to get home to see my friends, I couldn't be stuck here any longer. I nodded as I hobbled back to my room so that I could hide myself under the duvet until they were gone; as soon as I heard the front door shut it was go time.

Having already packed my required travelling items I headed to the limo as soon as I knew theirs had already driven away. I was aware of the fact that Mum and Dad would not be happy about me leaving, I was hoping my parents would calm down once I got back home and explained my reasons. What choice did they leave me anyway? They were the ones hiding deep dark secrets!

To my surprise Cliff was waiting at the door of the limousine outside, before I had a chance to ask him what was going on my new phone received a text. This is what it said:

JEAN: By now I'm sure you will have noticed Cliff standing in front of your getaway vehicle, Milo kindly rang me to inform me of your intention to flee back to America. I am sure I must be part of the reason, learning the truth like that cannot have been easy. There is more to the story and I would hate for me to die before you received the answers you deserve, travel safely in my private plane but please return to the Mansion before we are home ourselves. Cliff will accompany you and take you anywhere you would like to go, this can be our little secret.

Yours Sincerely

Jean (your grandmother)

I was very perplexed, this woman who had rapidly begun dominating my life seemed far cleverer than she acted. I waved awkwardly in Cliff's direction. His face was stern, he said nothing whilst walking towards a small plane. I decided to follow him due to the fact that I had little choice in the matter. On the upside it meant I could go to America and see Patricia. Who was I to squabble over how I made it to my desired destination?

Chapter Twenty-Two

The thought of being able to arrive in style had me feeling a little giddy. I looked around at my flying limousine and decided to lay down, it would be hours before we landed so I may as well get comfortable. I fell asleep quite unintentionally, the pillow was just so plush. By the time I woke up we had already reached America. I slept for hours with a peaceful dreamless sleep. The pilot's loud voice coming through the speaker was what woke me. We would apparently be landing shortly.

The thought of finally being back on American soil had me overjoyed. After Cliff helped me exit the plane we got straight into yet another limousine which was already at the airport waiting for us.

"Hey my name is Scott, I'll be your driver today. Where can I take you?"

It was good to hear an American accent again.

"Do you know where Lake Clair Park is?"

I was in a hurry to make my appearance.

"Sure thing miss I'll take you straight there if you like?"

Cliff shook his head in disagreement.

I was about to complain when I saw him place a wad of cash into my hands.

"Um... No, actually can you take me to a fancy store on the way please, a Mall maybe?"

Scott laughed heartily.

"I know just the one."

I had never enjoyed shopping before but maybe because I could never spend any money while doing so. Today was a different story, I intended on spending my money very unwisely indeed.

My mouth was agape, I had never witnessed such a wide range of gorgeous clothing. Scott called over one of the workers.

"Hey there Miss, this girl has got to look nice for a party. Can you get her all suited and booted please?"

I had no words that could describe the sheer thrill of these shop assistants fawning all over me.

"Eek, I love all of these! I'm going to try them on."

After a long time trying on clothes I had finally decided on which ones I wanted to wear as well as the ones I would be taking home.

"Okay, I'm done, where to next?"

Scott laughed at me.

"Do you want to get a little pampered too? Hair, makeup maybe? How about the *whole* shebang."

I did have time and that was a very irresistible offer.

How great would it be to turn up at the lake party and actually fit in with everyone for a change?

"Okay, let's do it."

I said with glee. I decided to be brave and let them cut some of my beloved hair off, the messy, long, tangled, brunette hair draped down my back; mistreated for too many years. The lovely ladies at the salon all fussed over me, however they only managed to save about half of my hair from extinction.

It was so amazing how flashing a bit of money had demanded such respect from people. I was starting to understand why the wealthier people who had been in my life had treated me the way that they did, my worn-down image was an eye sore to them.

I now had a shiny coat to my shoulder length hair, who knew fancy shampoo could add body and bounce? After they finished styling it we went to get my nails and makeup done. My nails were being painted a baby pink colour to match my rose coloured chiffon dress. I paired it with these adorable kitten heels, matching handbag and jewellery all with the same colour scheme.

My outfit had me looking just like a doll, even my make up matched my outfit whilst showing off cheekbones I never knew I had. Feeling confident with the choices I made, all I had to do now was surprise my best friend.

I had never felt so important before, maybe living in England with Grandma Jean wouldn't be as bad as I had originally thought. I should give her a chance to tell me her truth, at least she wanted to tell me her secrets. My parents clearly were hiding the truth from me, they had been my whole life.

I couldn't trust them even if they did suddenly grow a conscience and speak up. Putting all those horrible thoughts aside I focused on what was important now, it was time to show Patricia the new and improved me, everyone would finally see me as one of them instead of a lost puppy.

Chapter Twenty-Three

Down at the lake I could see Patricia attached to Tyler at the hip as usual, they seemed to be enjoying themselves immensely (without me). Much to my surprise, sitting at the table with them was my arch nemesis Cynthia Arnold. To catch you up, Cynthia Arnold was a girl from my elementary school, we had been sworn enemies ever since she pulled my skirt down in the fourth grade; I was called 'pants McGee' for the rest of the year. Cynthia thought she was 'it' but she was just a big bully.

Patricia had originally been in her group of friends, she had taken pity on me, the girl bravely chose my friendship over Cynthia's. I could not believe that Cynthia had the nerve to worm her way back into my friends' good graces! Not on my watch, I was going to put an end to this once and for all. Look at me now compared to back then, I was so much better than fourth grade me; I was going to show her that she couldn't force Patricia to be her friend just because I was visiting England.

Once we had parked close enough I swung the limo door wide open so all eyes would be fixated on me as I exited my first-class ride. Patricia stared right at me without any recognition on her face, even my best friend could not recognise that it was in fact me. I had to help her, she had suffered a lot from Cynthia's wrath over the years because of me.

It was my turn to play heroine, I was going to choose Patricia's friendship over everything including my family drama. It was the least I could do. I knew Cynthia was up to no good, she always had an ulterior motive behind every choice she had ever made.

Walking up to where they were sitting was terrifying and thrilling all at the same time.

"Hey Patz. Tyler, how's the hair?"

Tyler's mouth fell to his knees while Patricia stood frozen by silence.

"It's me guys, didn't you miss me? Why is that witch here at *our* Lake Party?"

I scowled in Cynthia's direction, this caused her to look up from the meaningless conversation that she was having with one of her nearby cronies.

"Pants McGee!"

Her maniacal grin sent a shiver down my spine.

Those two words had sent me straight back to the fourth grade.

"So sorry, I didn't recognise you under all that *paint* you're wearing, is that to help hide your ugly face?"

Cynthia spat out her venomous words and they shot right into my confidence bringing me down to my knees inside, I felt only two inches tall. Thankfully Patricia came to my rescue.

"Gail, let's go talk over here."

She must have come to the conclusion that it was time for some 'girl talk' one on one. I tried so hard to hide my self pity.

Patricia saw the tears welling up in my eyes.

"Why didn't you let me know you were coming?"

I stared right at her.

"Why is that *dragon* here!?"

Patricia sighed impatiently.

"I didn't know you were coming, I thought you would be in England and it wouldn't matter."

I was ablaze with jealousy, anger and confusion.

"That doesn't make any sense, you haven't talked to her in years so why would me being in England give her a reason to be at *our* party?"

What little was left of my composure and poise was now shattered into a million pieces.

Patricia began to reveal the disgustingly painful truth.

"Actually, we have been in touch more and more lately. We are becoming good friends again, I was going to tell you, but with everything you were going through I thought you wouldn't be able to 'handle it'."

Her air quotes were insulting to say the least, my arms flew into the air.

"How long have you two been 'friends' behind my back!?"

I mirrored her insulting air quotes.

Patricia was taken aback by my reaction.

"Look, it isn't a big deal! We have only been speaking for about six months now. Like I said, you *should* have let me know you were coming!"

Patricia appeared to be a little embarrassed by my display of emotions, not that this was unusual. To be fair, her parents had now begun to show interest in all of the commotion. I had never been good at hiding my emotions, I was a 'wear your heart on your sleeve' kind of a girl. If I knew then what I did now perhaps I would have kept my heart hidden and away from harm.

Fury was the emotion rearing its ugly head at this moment in time.

"So, It's my fault for trying to surprise *my* best friend, is it? I made the mistake of thinking you would be missing me, I wanted to cheer you up. I *thought* you didn't like Cynthia because of how she treated me!"

Patricia laughed out loud. Clearly I had been mistaken.

With my soul now crushed I had nothing left to lose.

"What? Over that pants thing? Come on big Gail, that was *years* ago, can't you just get over it!? That's all water under the bridge now."

I shrieked out loud.

"PANTS THING? GET OVER IT? She embarrassed me in front of the *entire* school AND videotaped it too! My parents had to take me to a shrink just so they could try and help me 'get over' it!"

She began looking around her shoulders nervously.

Patricia, at this stage, had decided that we were not far enough away from the party. She pulled me even further away into the bushes that were surrounding the lake. My shouting at the top of my lungs was potentially the cause.

"Gail, stop overreacting, I think you should *calm* down. You're embarrassing me. Cynthia is *my* friend and if you can't be nice, well, then maybe YOU are the one that *shouldn't* have come here."

Each word was a new nail in my coffin. The words went into my ears but my brain just couldn't process what I was hearing.

I have been sitting in this girl's shadow for far too long, idolising her while thinking I owed my life to her. In reality all I ever was to her was an embarrassment, a 'charity case', a doormat even!

"Did you *ever* care that I wasn't going to be here over the summer or was it just a relief? Were you actually glad that you and the wicked witch could *finally* be friends without worrying about me ruining it for you?"

I folded my arms attempting to hold in the sadness that had taken over me.

Patricia spoke without hesitation.

"It was more of a relief, yes, you have been *awfully* clingy lately. You're always moaning about some drama, Cynthia gets me, she listens to me and doesn't bother me with any of her *boring* home life."

Her words hit me like a spear to my chest. Until this moment I thought the exact same thing of my friendship with Patricia, but now my rose tinted glasses had been forcibly removed seeing things a little clearer.

While I stood impaled by an emotional harpoon all she did was walk away from me, only turning around to push the weapon in further.

"Just for the record Gail, I agree with Cynthia, you *do* look like a 'wannabe pop star' in that ridiculous get up. A bit of makeup can't hide the *real* you, you're still the same annoying fourth grader that I met all those years ago; a *pathetic* loser."

This time she spoke for the benefit of her new found posse. In that moment my entire world crumbled around me and I was left in a never-ending oblivion, I wasn't going to let them laugh at my expense any more.

I raced back to the limousine where Cliff and Scott were waiting for me, it was no good, the tears couldn't be held back any longer. In my complete devastation a hand reached out with a handkerchief extending from it, I used it to wipe my tears away. Scott, a complete stranger, had shown me more compassion in the five minutes I had known him than Patricia had throughout our entire friendship.

"My 'so-called' friend just tore me to shreds."

Something in the drivers eyes showed me he too was no stranger to pain.

I glanced at Cliff, he seemed to be uninterested in my emotional meltdown.

"Don't worry girl, they don't deserve you! Now give us a smile."

Scott spoke encouragingly as I smiled weakly.

"That's it girly, you look *beautiful*, don't let them tell you any different; they're just jealous!"

I nodded briefly.

"Can we go back to England now? I don't think me and America were 'meant to be' somehow."

Scott sped full force all the way to the airport.

Cliff helped me take all of my bags of shopping onto the plane. Looking at my new wardrobe only served to worsen my pain. No amount of money in the world would ever make me good enough for the likes of Patricia.

Even my drama at home had to be better than being berated by a pint size human, someone who I *thought* had my back. Who did she think she was, belittling me like that? I didn't need her anymore, maybe Grandma Jean would let me stay with her, that way I would never have to go back to Atlanta ever again.

Chapter Twenty-Four

The rest of my week was pretty dull, the only thing I could do was get to know my cousin Juliette Robinson. She wasn't so bad, I found out during our conversations that we had a lot of common interests. Not only does she love music, Juliette also wasn't very popular at school. I shared some of my trade secrets when it came to taking care of spots, the cream I gave her was working nicely. Her face was looking less spotty by the day.

Juliette was mature for her age so despite her being in the year below me at school, she could easily fool people into thinking she was my age. I now knew tons of cool new English hairstyles, we tried trading some of our clothes although we were far apart in sizes. What Juliette lacked in height she made up for in girth and vice versa with me. She seemed to love being in my company, never having another sibling is what initially bonded us. We understood each other in a unique only-child way.

I always wondered what it would be like growing up with a sibling, time with Juliette gave me a glimpse into what life would have been like with her as my sister. She made me feel a little less on my own than I had previously felt before. She was in the middle of talking about how different our schools were, I tried hard to stay interested however curiosity was definitely getting the better of me. I waited on tenterhooks for my opportunity to change topics, I had to find a way to be subtly inquisitive. Not an easy task.

I desperately wanted to find out more about my family's deep dark secrets, Juliette was currently my only link to discovering anything new. Her parents clearly knew more than they were letting on, it was possible Juliette Robinson did too. I had to try, I quickly used the thirty seconds of silence as a way to creep my question into our conversation.

"Julz..."

She loved it when I shortened her name.

"...does my mum have a brother?"

Juliette seemed to clam up upon hearing my question.

"Um, yeah I *think* so."

She was most certainly hiding something from me.

I used our new found friendship in order to coax information out of her.

"Come on, I thought we were friends who told each other *everything*... I shared all of *my* secrets."

Juliette began to wince in response to the severe pout on my face.

"Promise you won't get mad?"

She looked a little scared, I used my finger to imitate a cross symbol.

"Cross my heart."

She still looked worried despite my sincere promise.

"Whatever I tell you has to stay between us."

Placing my hand on her I reassured her further that it would be our secret.

Juliette, seeming pensive, stared deeply into my eyes but only for a moment.

"Okay, I trust you... I'll tell you what I know."

I pulled her in for a squeeze.

"Thanks cuz."

She inhaled deeply before revealing all.

"I overheard my parents talking about you coming to stay, they were talking a lot about your parents. I didn't catch the whole conversation but I did hear one thing that sounded a bit odd."

Her brief pause caused a lump to develop in my throat.

I was terrified of hearing what she might have to say.

"My mum said to my dad these words 'she is my sister and he is my brother, we all lived in the same house together, so how can I just *accept* their marriage? It's not normal' the rest was muffled so I don't know what else was said."

Her face was full of anguish. I tried my hardest to digest the information she had just fed me. If only you could buy medicine for emotional indigestion.

I tried hard to stay positive.

"It could mean anything, maybe your dad lived here after they married?"

That was Juliette's poor attempt at rationalising an unbearable truth.

"No, they eloped while pregnant with me, at least that is the story they told me."

The expression on Juliette's face only worsened. I began thinking of all the excuses that could rationalise this information. Despite my best efforts I couldn't think of many reasons that could make this okay.

I decided that denial was my best option.

"You probably misheard them. I mean, they are siblings by marriage so no doubt that's what she meant! I would be all kinds of deformed if my parents were related!"

I scoffed at my own words, I was half laughing at this dire news. I truly wished I had never asked anyone about anything. I wanted to crawl inside a box marked special delivery to anywhere but here. My only coping mechanism was humour so mocking the fact that incest was the reason that I was alive was my only choice of survival.

Juliette had found her smile again which was amazing to see.

"Maybe you need to confront your parents and ask them once and for all what is going on. Just don't mention me... my parents would kill me!"

We shook on it to seal the deal, if I was going to get to the bottom of this ever-worsening horror story that was turning out to be my life then I would have to play them at their own game. It's not like I would be doing things any different to them. I'd love to pretend that I was better than these insidious creatures raising me but the truth was I wanted answers, no matter what it cost to my integrity.

My parents weren't about to admit that they were related now were they? No, I had to find out for myself, as much as Jean seemed intent on revealing the truth to me I wasn't sure if I could trust her either. Her trickery over the flight to Atlanta still left me shaking in my boots, she was no dithering, elderly woman that was for certain. Grandma Jean definitely had her wits about her so I would have to use my smart, little mind to devise a set of events that would lead to the truth having to come out, whether they liked it or not.

Before the rest of our family had arrived back home Juliette was able to lend me some recording equipment, we assembled (in secret) some small microphones and cameras all over the house; I wanted to catch them in the act of their deceit so that they could no longer fob me off with falsities. Juliette was the only one who knew about it, we didn't place them anywhere inappropriate. I did not want to be scarred for life, I just wanted the truth. Although I wasn't so sure I could do one without the other. Unfortunately, this would mean that the footage would be limited.

It was only a matter of time before someone slipped up or felt the need to talk about the real story behind how I came to live in America; without my estranged wealthy family members who lived in England. Juliette's parents used them to spy on the nanny's that were used over the years, they had been idle ever since, we even had stuffed bear cams dotted around the place; we made sure they would be unnoticed by the residents of Grandma Jean's Mansion. Now all we had to do was sit patiently and wait.

Chapter Twenty-Five

About two weeks into my investigation our luck came in while we were braiding each other's hair in my room. I'd taken to hiding in my room with Juliette, we would scour through footage any chance we got. So far we had found nothing, on the off chance that the live footage proved useful I would always have the laptop open. You never know when an interesting conversation could transpire, it just so happens that all our waiting was now worth it.

It was our mothers who were the culprits, it seemed innocent at first. My mother called over her sister, it was in the east wing in Grandma Jean's massive estate.

"Sis, wait up will you?"

My mother seemed anxious to speak with her.

"What is it Deidre?"

It was clear that Christina had no interest in speaking with her sister.

"I just need to know you aren't going to tell Abigail any details regarding William and..."

Christina interrupted Deidre before she could finish her sentence.

Her next words horrified me.

"Details about your sordid little love affair you mean? No dear Sister, I wouldn't dream of it. You and our adopted brother William can stay in your pathetic excuse for a marriage just don't expect me to be celebrating your wedding anniversary any time soon!"

With that Aunt Christina stormed off down the corridor leaving my sobbing mother in her wake. I couldn't believe it, and probably wouldn't have if I hadn't heard it with my own two ears.

So my dad *was* my Uncle, that's who Grandma Jean must have been referring to. He had to have been the Uncle who took my mother to the abortion clinic. My parents were brother and sister after all but via adoption not by blood. Which would explain why I didn't have webbed feet at least, this also meant that both my parents planned to get rid of me; until Jean forced them not to. Juliette gazed at me as if to say 'wow' so I just nodded in agreement, I couldn't find the words that would even begin to describe how I was feeling at that moment.

Juliette interrupted my pit of silence.

"Things could be worse Abby, you could have my parents."

I laughed out loud, Juliette's parents were the picture of perfection compared to mine.

"No seriously, they aren't fun to be around, they are always moaning at me and shouting at each other, at least your parents get along."

Juliette whimpered as she tried to convince me that her life was worse than mine.

"Julz, come on... they aren't *that* bad."

Juliette just shrugged my words off of her shoulders.

Aunty Christina was headed our way, I quickly closed the laptop before she reached our door. She was just there to let us know that dinner was ready. We both headed off to the dining room, my mind wandered onto what might be awaiting us on the dinner table.

This little adventure I had been dragged into left much to be desired however the food was so unlike anything I had ever eaten before. Some nights it was escargot while others it was beef wellington which I detested. My favourite dish so far had to be toad in the hole. Who wouldn't like yummy sausages cooked in golden batter?

Chapter Twenty-Six

Tonight we were eating tomato and basil soup with croutons, rack of lamb with dauphinoise potatoes and caramelised pears with greek yogurt. It was nearly enough to distract me from my real purpose at the dinner table that evening. The task at hand was far too important, Juliette and I had rehearsed our script a few hundred times over; with a variety of different options depending on what was said in return. I just needed the right opening in order to be able to sneak in our practised conversation.

My father was trying to be chatty so when he asked us whether we had been up to anything interesting lately I saw a way in. As soon as he mentioned my name it was go time.

"Oh, well…"

I paused briefly until I had been able to get Juliette's attention, I gave her the signal by stroking my left eyebrow with my pinky.

"…funny you should ask that Dad, I have been reading a lot of English literature lately."

My dad raised his eyebrows with delight as he prompted me for some more information just as I suspected he would.

His naive response showed he did not know what was coming his way.

"Oh yeah, how different are they to our classic American novels?"

I had to say this next line perfectly in order for it to have the effect that I needed it to.

"Well, they are *quite* different, the one I have just finished reading is all about illegitimate marriages and teenage pregnancies, it concluded with this major debate about abortions and whether or not they should be made illegal."

My mum quite literally spat out her food upon hearing this sentence.

She hurriedly tried to defuse the bomb I had just lit.

"Don't you think that *might* be above your age Abby dear?"

Poor Deidre frantically tried to change the subject.

"No Mum, I think it is *quite* poignant and relevant in society today, don't you think Juliette?"

This was her cue to backup my statement in order to make it seem like an innocent coincidence to our situation.

"Why yes Abigail, I agree, there are a lot of girls who struggle with a decision on keeping a child or not. There are also some who are forced into marriages with their relatives all over the world."

My mother excused herself from the dinner table while all the other guilty parties remained silent.

Weirdly Grandma Jean had a sinister gleam to her face as if this was just what she wanted to happen. Our precision to the whole act worked marvellously, my mother was feeling guilty and was surely going to have to talk to someone about the whole thing. That's when I would be waiting, my only hope was that it would be in a room where I had some cameras hidden.

My parents still believed that I was unaware of their horrid secret, this meant they also had no reason to suspect foul play, it wouldn't be long until I had enough dirt on *all* of them; then I could face them without any conceivable way for them to lie their way out of it.

I could hear muffled noises coming from a nearby space on my way back to my bedroom, I returned hastily to my laptop in order to check if my cameras were picking up the conversation. It was my mum, she was in the green room talking with Grandma Jean.

"This is such a mess Mum! I have to tell her the truth, I can't keep hiding things from her."

My mother was distraught.

"No Deidre, if you do that she will just hate you, you don't want her knowing that you and William are both my children *and* that you tried to abort her."

How is it that my grandma can pretend to my face that she wants me to know the truth and then convince my mother to keep quiet?

At least I now know Jean isn't to be trusted either.

"Mum, come on, what choice did I have? You were threatening to take my baby away from me, I was just a scared kid and you knew I liked William *before* you adopted him! Don't pretend you didn't just adopt him to keep us apart. I tried Mum, we both did but we really loved each other and *still* do."

Jean remained quiet, clearly calculating her next move.

"We didn't mean to get pregnant and I wasn't going to let you take her away from us either. I'm not ashamed of my love for William, I am ashamed that I have lied to Abigail for so very long. If you weren't dying none of this would be happening and we would still be living a happy life together."

At that moment I saw my mum in a new light.

She was a brave woman for standing up to her mother like this.

"You robbed fourteen years of knowing my granddaughter Deidre, your silly Speech won't save you nor will telling your daughter the truth, she will hate *you* just as you hate *me*; I will make sure of it even if it's the last thing I do!"

After I heard those nasty words Jean had said I knew my mum was never the enemy, that witch of a grandma was.

My mum stormed out of the room in tears, now was my time to confront her once and for all. Leaving my room in a hurry I ran down to meet her before she had a chance to get too far away. I grabbed her suddenly.

"Abby what is it? Where are you taking me?"

I just pulled her faster and shushed her as we entered my room.

"Shh Mum, quick, come into my room so I can explain."

With that I locked us inside my room and waited for my grandma to retire to her own bedroom.

My mum was staring at my open laptop.

"Are you going to tell me what's going on now?"

I peered deep into my mother's eyes and I saw the scared little teenager inside of her begging to be loved.

"I love you Mum, I know everything and I forgive you. I had planned on a big 'surprise reveal' where I made you feel bad for lying but I see now that you didn't have a choice. I also see that we have a bigger problem than the secret of where I came from."

Deidre was lost for words and didn't know how to fathom what I was saying.

I showed her the camera footage that I had stored on my computer.

"How long have you been spying on me?"

She seemed impressed alongside her obvious feelings of surprise.

"Long enough to know that William, my dad, is your adopted brother. I also know you tried to have me aborted along with the fact that your mum is evil and *needs* to be stopped once and for all."

My mum fell onto the bed, she sat with her head in her hands.

"It's okay Mum, just tell me your side of the story, I won't hate you. I know you love me."

I sat next to her and placed my hand on her shoulder as she sighed deeply, she lifted her head and agreed to tell me everything.

Chapter Twenty-Seven

Deidre raised herself up and started pacing back and forth.

"William was such a genial boy, we went to school together briefly, did you know that, Abby?"

I shook my head gently.

"Yes, he was such a handsome, strong boy who had the world at his feet."

She chuckled softly to herself, she was so clearly filled with regret.

"He was an exchange student from America, his parents were wealthy, actually they were business partners with my parents."

She spoke with a subtle frailty in her voice.

I allowed her time to get her words out.

"They had asked that my mother take him in for the fall every year, this was so that he was able to get a first hand experience of life in the UK."

A smile spread across her face.

"It was love at first sight, I was about your age when we met, his loud outward appearance left him looking so carefree. I had lived a life of

solitude in this massive Mansion with a sister who hated me and a mother who belittled me every chance she got."

Her smile quickly vanished.

I couldn't imagine how hard it must have been.

"My dad was my only friend, however he was always busy working. While William was in the UK we spent every waking moment together, my mother knew we liked each other and complained to my father about it on many occasions. He of course was the only thing standing in my mother's warpath."

She glanced at me, I shared a knowing look with her. Grandma Jean had proved herself to be a cold, calculated, extremely intelligent woman. I can't imagine it was easy to fool her.

Deidre's voice grew shaky.

"Unfortunately there was an accident, one year William's parents and my father were travelling to Canada on a business trip, Grandma Jean would

never stand for flying in a 'chopper' so she refused to join them."

My mum stood by the window. She separated the curtains whilst looking outside longingly with clenched fists.

"It was a day much like today when we heard the news, a day like any other..."

Her voice trailed off in an eerie fashion, I wanted to hold her and tell her it was okay but I knew it truly wasn't.

I waited patiently for her to continue, she stared intently outside as if she were looking for something but I knew she was trying to stop herself from crying.

"William and I were in the library studying when Cliff came to fetch us. The news hit him like a ton of bricks, just as it did to me too. His parents, along with my father, had died in a horrific helicopter accident."

I couldn't believe what I was hearing. She was silent for some time, I wanted to run to her but I felt if I stood up my legs would turn to jelly so I remained sitting.

My mother unclenched her fists before drawing the curtains firmly shut.

"William was all I had left in this world, I too was all he had left. My mother decided to do the honourable thing and adopt him, his sister didn't want to live in England and used the shares of her father's company left to her in the will as leverage to emancipate herself. Jean paid for the shares and with that money now hers the court allowed her to be legally responsible for herself. William could have easily gone to live with her but I knew he stayed for me."

I could see now which parent Heather took after. Mum stared right at me with a pain in her eyes. I had no response to offer her, although I wish I could take the pain away, I had no idea how.

She bravely continued with her story.

"Grandma Jean forbade us from being together ever again, she said we were to act as real siblings, we tried very hard to follow her orders. However, one night the grief took over us, in doing so one thing led to another and we fell pregnant with you."

Her barely noticeable smile returned.

Although it was brief I knew it had been there to reassure me that I was the only good thing to come out of this mess.

"I was terrified of my mother and saw no other way out, I could try and keep it a secret or go for an abortion. William wanted to keep you and said we should run away together, he tried to convince me we would be fine."

That sounded like my dad.

"Grandma Jean had both of our family's money so all we had for help was his sister in America; she was more than willing to help us escape my mother."

Which explains how we ended up in America.

She kept going, her tears seemed to have stopped for now.

"Mum found out somehow and tried to force me to go to a convent and wait to have you there, but that meant you would be raised as my sister. I was sixteen when I fell pregnant with you, I was just a kid Abby, Cliff helped us escape from the prison of this awful building, he snuck us out in the middle of the night and flew us to Chicago where William's sister now lives."

I was surprised to hear that Cliff, the loyal lapdog of Grandma Jean, was their saviour; he seemed to have a lot of secrets.

I was curious about one thing.

"How come it took Grandma Jean so long to find you?"

I was extremely surprised by all of this, such drama and utter wickedness had ensued.

"We changed our surnames and moved to a place where she didn't have any contacts as far as we knew. We kept hidden for as long as we could, I honestly thought we had gotten away with it."

My mum got down on her knees.

I felt nervous as she looked me straight in the eyes and cupped her hands around mine.

"I love you Abby, I am so glad I never went through with the abortion, my life without you just wouldn't be worth it."

I smiled a wide smile as I grabbed my mum tightly.

"Mum I know you love me, I love you too... I think we should move here. We should try to get dirt on your mum to finally be holding all of the cards..."

My mum gaped, showing her concern.

She interrupted me mid sentence.

"Why would you want to move here? What happened Abby?"

I turned away from her piercing gaze.

"Nothing, I...well...I realised that I have no reason to go back there anymore. I like it here, Juliette and I have become close, the school sounds pretty cool and we don't have a reason to hide anymore."

My mum knew there was something I wasn't telling her but chose not to push me on the subject.

After a moment's pause she decided to entertain my idea.

"Okay, say we did move out here, how on earth would we manage to trap my mum into revealing her secrets?"

I winked at her.

"My cameras of course, I found *your* secrets out didn't I? All we have to do is pretend to hate each other and Grandma Jean will think that her plan has worked. She is bound to slip up one way or another."

Deidre agreed to my plan. We had no reason to go back to Atlanta, the time for running was over, it was now time to fight.

Chapter Twenty-Eight

I sat my parents down so we could have a real conversation, we needed to figure out what we were going to do. After some debating we all came to the conclusion that we needed to sell our house in Atlanta and move here. It would give us time to say goodbye to everyone, although I did secretly hope Patricia's family wouldn't be invited.

My mum and dad had mentioned that it would be a good idea to go visit Patricia, Tyler and company while we were back home, they were still unaware of our falling out. I chose not to bring it up, it would be good to see her one last time even under these circumstances; there was a lot still to be said between us.

I'm not sure if she wanted to speak to me, Patricia had made it clear I meant nothing to her. She had humiliated me in front of my mortal enemy, our long standing friendship had been demolished in a blink of an eye. Yet, I still wanted to know if she truly was this monster I had been exposed to back at the lake.

There was still a small ember of hope buried deep under a smokey fog of anger towards her. Mostly I just wanted to rub it in her face that I got to live in a fancy mansion. I was her equal now whether or not she ever treated me as such.

I went online just to see if she had tried to get in touch with me, she hadn't, in fact I had been removed as a contact. Seeing the blank space where her name used to be in my favourite contacts was like a needle in my eye, it just goes to show just how little she cared about me to begin with. I know I could never just wake up and decide that the girl who sat next to me on the bus every morning was not worthy of friendship anymore.

Although, come to think of it, that is kind of what I did by not trying to fight for our friendship. She might be sorry for how she behaved, maybe Cynthia was bullying her into being mean to me, I began to imagine all the different scenarios that could ensue. It was more than likely I was just trying to believe in the impossible.

I had far more experience with imaginary conversations than I did with real ones, so much so that I sometimes find it hard to distinguish between the real and fake ones. Hence why I loved the characters in my books far more than real life humans.

Unfortunately memories of reality hit me like a wave of destruction which sent me spiralling out of control.

"Mum…"

She was busy sorting out our flight plans.

"Have you invited Patricia?"

Without even looking up she replied.

"Is there a reason why I shouldn't?"

I knew she was on to me.

"I just don't think she wants to come, she will be busy."

She furrowed her brow before looking at me.

"What is going on Abby? Did you and Patricia fall out?"

I finally caved and 'spilled my guts'.

I revealed all, including my secret trip to Atlanta.

"Okay fine, yes… I went to Atlanta behind your back with your mum's help. In doing so I interrupted a beautiful get together with Cynthia and Patricia…"

My rant was stopped by a hug from my mother.

"It'll be fine Abby, I know you don't like Cynthia but they were friends first and maybe it's time to bury the hatchet."

The cross look on my face did not deter my parents' enthusiasm over ruining my life yet again.

My mother hadn't finished yet.

"How about I invite Cynthia along too, it would be a shame to lose your friend."

I didn't even have the words to defend myself, there was no end to the amount of wrong that suggestion was.

Looks like even with the truth out in the open I did not get off scot-free, I had to endure another encounter with the spoiled brats; one of which was once my friend. I just reassured myself that I wasn't worth their time. No way would they turn up just to make my life more miserable than it already was.

Juliette was concerned about me going back to Atlanta, she thought that I may never come back. In order to reassure her I made us matching friendship bracelets for the purposes of reassuring her that this was not the case.

"Don't worry *nothing* can affect our friendship, I will be back in no time."

The bright coloured fibres intertwined into a plait.

"Thanks Abby, I'll wear it all the time."

Juliette smiled shyly as she twisted her bracelet back at forth, I embraced her briefly before we headed off to dinner.

Cliff was due to fly us to Atlanta in the morning, Grandma Jean had handled the news graciously even though I knew that she had wanted us to move here from the start. We had all been sitting around the dinner table when my mother announced the news.

"We have decided to move in with you Mum as we are needed here more than back in Atlanta."

She had said this bravely while her mum stared at her blankly. In reply Jean had said.

"If that is what you wish, Deidre."

I mean even the ice queen herself would have offered a warmer response. Grandma Jean wasn't one for familiarities however she was extremely crafty and was never to be underestimated.

Cliff helped us board the private plane fit for royalty, my mum was so surprised at how inviting the interior was, Dad looked like a dandelion in a field of daisies with his psychedelic shirt and matching shorts.

"Are you looking forward to seeing your sister again Dad? Won't you miss her when we move back to England?"

Dad just gazed at me with only one eyebrow raised.

"Don't worry darling. We will still see your Aunt Angela, not forgetting your second favourite cousin Heather, from time to time."

My dad winked at me.

He knew full well how much I detested Heather.

"Yeah, she is my *only* other cousin, Dad. You could just as easily say my least favourite cousin yet she'd still rank the same."

I huffed in his direction.

"Do we really have to go see them on this trip?"

I tried my best to escape the company of my horrible cousin.

"Don't be silly Abby, you have to say goodbye to Robert, Heather and Angela! They are family after all, you are too quick to sever relationship ties with people when they upset you."

My dad seemed unimpressed with my outburst.

I know he was having a dig over my fall out with Patricia, they didn't seem to understand that I wasn't the cause of our now ended friendship. That's without mentioning that the reason behind my ease of walking away from family potentially ran in the family. I wasn't about to start a war with the only people I had left in my life.

"Okay Dad, I'm sorry, she just gets on my nerves that's all."

My mum and dad embraced me in a three way hug as they reassured me that the trip was going to be immensely fun.

Chapter Twenty-Nine

I was dreading the flight until a surprise guest decided to join us for our trip, as I turned around to the entrance of the plane Juliette could be seen standing next to Cliff.

Since the first time I saw her she had slimmed down a bit and blemishes on her face had started fading away, she had settled on wearing contacts which meant that her pretty face was starting to show through more and more. She stood awkwardly fidgeting with her bracelet and smiled in my direction, she was wearing a purple dress with sunflowers on it. I couldn't help but think how nice she looked.

I grinned with anticipation.

"Is it okay if I join you Abby? I've never been to America before."

I leapt out of my chair and ran to greet my cousin, embracing her with force.

"Yay, of course you can Julz, I *need* the company."

Juliette became more relaxed upon hearing my enthusiasm over her joining us. At least I wouldn't have to face Patricia or Heather alone anymore.

"You are going to love it there, I can show you our doll-sized house and you can share my matchbox of a bedroom."

Juliette laughed at me.

"It can't be that bad, surely."

I changed my face to match my statement of fact with raised eyebrows.

"You wanna bet?"

I laughed for effect. I was ready for Atlanta, bring it on!

I started telling her all about the residence including information about our neighbourhood. The flight went by in no time at all with some in-flight movies and also the great company of my even greater cousin.

"So why did your parents decide to let you come with us?"

I queried Juliette.

"They said that they had some important matters to attend to and I guess it was better to not have me around in order to do it."

I paused for a moment.

"Well I haven't deactivated my cameras yet so maybe we can find out what they were up to when we get back."

Juliette liked the sound of that.

Her parents had been fighting a lot lately, even I had started noticing the rift between them. She was worried they might be breaking up, she would more than likely live with her mum and barely see her dad anymore. Juliette got on far better with her dad than her mum. Aunt Christina was a difficult person to be around, I never felt at ease around her. I reassured her they would be fine but I too became concerned about them splitting up, they seemed to detest each other.

Our first stop in Atlanta was our minuscule abode, we unpacked and got settled in.

"Wow, Abby, you weren't lying. This 'house' is like a box compared to Grandma's Mansion, but I like it, it's very quaint."

Her condescending tone of voice was ignored as I knew it was unintentional.

"Well this is how I've lived my whole life, I'm sure you can cope for just a week or two. You may not

have your own bathroom here, but who needs your own bathroom when you can share it with the whole house?"

Her smile dropped.

"Are you *serious*? We have to share a bathroom?"

The horror on her face was priceless.

I couldn't help but burst into a fit of giggles.

"Your face says it all, you're going to *love* it here."

I set up the bedroom with a mattress on the floor covered in bedding.

"I am NOT sleeping on *that!*"

Juliette became distraught.

"Don't worry, *queen* Julz, you get the bed; I'll take the mattress."

I did a quick bow before getting a pillow thrown at me. As much as she seemed to hate her new living quarters, I was very glad to have her here with me. She was fast becoming my favourite person.

My mum had cooked my favourite dish, Mac, Bac and Cheese, Juliette had a face like a screw up tissue as she pushed it around the plate.

"Come on Julz, give it a try you won't regret it."

Juliette sighed and tasted a bit.

"Mmm delicious, I can most certainly taste the calories."

Juliette was very unhappy with her weight. She felt as though she were a pig in a pen, trotting around the place. I kept telling her that she looked fine and weight doesn't matter but she was determined to diet and get 'as skinny as me' (her words, not mine).

I didn't feel that I was skinny but I guess standing next to Juliette I would look slim, when she complained about her weight I would remind her of my broad man shoulder and lack of curves but she just saw me as a tall, pretty, thin girl that she would much rather be than herself.

"Julz I have told you before and I will tell you again, you are fine just as you are."

She muttered under her breath that maybe she wasn't happy with being 'fine' before flashing me a small smile.

Juliette pushed the plate away.

"Sorry Aunt Deidre it is delicious but I don't have the appetite to eat it, at the moment."

My mum smiled kindly.

"Shall I make something different Juliette? I can do a 'low cal' chicken salad for you, if you would prefer?"

Juliette graciously accepted her offer and ate her rabbit food quite happily. I chose to ignore her snide remark, she was clearly having issues and my compliments weren't working.

I may not like my figure but I wasn't going to complain about it, I know it could be worse, I had just started getting breasts and I was growing into my shoulders more and more these days. I resolved to take Juliette shopping in order to cheer her up, like Jean had enabled me to do, I asked if I could get Juliette a makeover. My mum approved of my plan and made arrangements for us to go to the Mall on the way to meet Heather and her family.

Juliette liked the idea of getting a makeover but was scared about how her parents would react.

"Come on Julz, they are too wrapped up in their own dramas, they might not even notice and you deserve a treat."

This seemed to reassure her, she had been put at ease now. I had never met a girl so insecure in herself, from my perspective there was no call for it, the girl had a lot of plus points to be proud of but she just saw her flaws. I was hoping with this trip I could help her to feel happy to be her, I wanted to show her that being big can be just as beautiful.

Chapter Thirty

On the way to Chicago we ended up stopping at this gigantic shopping Mall filled to the rafters with stores, there wasn't a thing you couldn't buy in *this* place. I took Juliette to a shop I personally loved but she didn't like it there, it was due to the fact that the size clothing she needed was in a separate section of the store, she was too embarrassed to root through the plus-size clothing.

I took her to another store where all the clothes were mixed in together and gathered a variety of dresses, jeans, shoes and tops for her to try on in the changing room; I waited outside as she did a fashion show of each item in turn.

She eventually picked a few outfits that she liked enough to buy, after that we moved on to hair and makeup. She didn't want her hair cut too short so as not to make her mother mad but she did have a trim and a style put into it; with makeup she appeared to be even prettier and much more grown up. I got her to wear a new outfit so that we could take some pictures together and post it onto social media, 'rolling with my bestie cousin Julz' was the title above the pictures that I had posted.

We made sure our matching friendship bracelets were showing in the pictures just to secure the fact that we were best buds, in case the cool friendship poses weren't enough to show that fact off to the masses. I don't know if we were such good friends due to the fact that we had no other choice or if we truly liked each other's company, this trip was most assuredly going to be the deciding vote on that one.

I liked the girl, no doubt, but we didn't really have much in common except a broken messed up family that we happened to be both connected to by blood; not forgetting our mutual love of music, of course. She had been there for me when I had no one else, the time when I had felt so completely alone, I just *had* to do the same for her now; it was literally the least I could do.

It felt good being the friend with it all together for a change, while needing to help her out I became the shoulder to cry on instead of being the one crying. It did make me feel bad for Patricia as I was probably the weight she was carrying around with her, back when we were friends, she must have felt obliged to help me sort my life out like I did with Juliette.

Maybe that's why she dumped me, it was because a better, more helpful friend came along. Someone who didn't need propping up, unlike me; Cynthia had now come back into her life which meant she no longer needed me anymore. I thought back to all the times that she had done things in order to cheer me up or make me feel better, I could only think of one genuine moment in our friendship where she seemed to really care about me.

The moment that I had remembered was the time that Cynthia had begun to bully me, *that* was when she first even noticed my existence, before that I was just a nobody walking around. I guess that I had always felt as if, because she had rescued me from that monster, that this in turn meant that I owed her my permanent loyalty.

She had kept me on a short leash, now that I had time to think clearly about the matter, she was only happy if I was doing things the way she had wanted me to; in fact I was never brave enough to challenge her (until I was told that I was visiting England).

For once I had a real drama of my own to face, all she had wanted to do was focus on how it had been affecting her, maybe we were never friends to begin with. Juliette had shown more care to my feelings and my needs than Patricia had in our entire friendship; I just hoped that our encounter with Heather goes better than how it normally goes. The dread of seeing Patricia was enough to cope with, I didn't need the added stress from having to deal with the 'stuck-up princess' as well.

Heather, as always, had her sour face perfectly covered in makeup, matching her outfit to a tee; she never

ever had a hair out of place (like it or not the girl was flawless). Perhaps that was part of the reason that I couldn't stand her, she was *too* perfect, it irritated me more than I cared to admit (even to myself).

I used to moan about her to Patricia, we would enjoy mocking her together; 'little miss know it all' we would call her or 'goody two shoes'. My favourite had to be 'stuck-up princess', unfortunately those memories are now tarnished with doubt and mistrust.

"Who's your 'gal pal' *Gail*?"

Heather said my name in a snarky tone of voice, I knew in her mind she was thinking 'Gail the Whale' (which still made no sense), the girl may have had her beauty but she wasn't very intelligent.

"This is our cousin, on my mum's side, *Heather.*"

I matched her tone of voice while saying her name.

Although I didn't have a mean rhyming nickname to go with it, mostly because it didn't rhyme with anything bad.

"So, not really *our* cousin, then is she?"

The look on her face said it all, she considered my mum and of our side of the family to not actually be a part of her family. Now that I know more about my side of the family I kind of understood her disdain, despite the sins of my grandmother and mother I hardly deserved hatred from her, I was an innocent bystander in my mother's womb when it all went down.

I am surprised however, that she hadn't used it as ammo to upset me before now, maybe she didn't know about it or perhaps she just relished in knowing something about my life that I didn't.

"If that is how you see it Heather, then fine, she is *my* cousin. *We* are visiting you to say goodbye, forever. I'm moving in with *my* family in the UK."

I emphasised the 'my' and 'we' to make sure that she was under no assumptions that I actually cared about her dislike of me and my side of the family.

"Good riddance to bad rubbish! Yeah, you *are* the bad rubbish."

Her sly smile didn't last long because just as she was insulting us her parents had walked into the room where we were all sitting.

"Heather, can you please use your manners with our guests?"

My Aunt Angela had decided to take it upon herself to let Heather know that she was listening in to our conversation. A fact I knew before she spoke yet failed to tell her about it, on purpose. It was about time she got caught out.

"Of course, Mum. Sorry."

The transition from snide to sincere in a matter of seconds was humorous to say the least.

Angela was as flawless as her daughter, her appearance was nothing like my dad, I was curious to behold what their parents looked like; even if only to distinguish where their differing features came from. When we get back to the UK, I will be sure to start investigating my family more. I wanted to see pictures of all the different members of my family; especially my grandfather.

We had a lovely few days with my dad's family, despite the vicious glares extending my way anytime Heather had the chance, the girl needed a new hobby.

Juliette was very quiet throughout our stay with the Millers, I didn't have a chance to speak with her in private, due to the fact that we were both sharing a room with Heather for the duration of our visit in Chicago.

We got to visit the local sites and show Juliette some lovely parts of America, which was nice. I couldn't wait to show her my favourite places in Atlanta. Heather, however, couldn't wait to see the back of both of us, the same went for me for that matter; we got away unscathed just about. Her words didn't phase me as I was very used to her by now, I just felt sorry that Juliette had to endure her loathing.

Back into the private plane we went, it was great flying in style from place to place but Cliff was a very silent man and chose not to stay with us, instead he preferred sleeping in the plane until he was needed again. To be fair the inside of the plane was nearly as big as my house in Atlanta, it had cabin quarters with sleeping areas so he was probably living in the lap of luxury. I couldn't decide what to do first when we got back, I couldn't even work out how we were going to fit it all in before having to go home.

Mum and Dad had to sell their house first, or at least set it in motion to be sold, before we were able to head back to the UK. The two of them also had to quit their jobs and arrange for all of our stuff to be sent to England via shipping containers, a task which had not been easy, we had to decide what we needed to keep and what we could do without.

I know it was asking a lot for them to move to England, now that Grandma Jean had been diagnosed with terminal cancer it wouldn't be long until she was bedridden, we needed to be close to her or she would never leave us alone.

It was time to stop letting that woman dictate what it was that we were going to do with our lives, she thought that she was winning but we would have the last laugh (if I manage to get my own way that is). My parents were only hiding out in America so that she wouldn't be able to find us and tell me the truth, now that is no longer an issue. So what reason do we have to stay in America anymore?

If we had close friends we were going to miss than maybe they wouldn't have agreed with me, the truth is that they have kept themselves closed in a box living in fear of their mother for the whole of their lives, they couldn't get close to people or they would find out the secrets they had hidden away; that was something that they just couldn't afford.

Maybe that is why I found it so hard to establish close relationships myself. I have never witnessed how to have a close friend before. I kept everyone at arm's length using humour to deflect their attention just long enough to prevent them breaching the walls that I surrounded myself in.

I was safe in the prison I had formed for myself, I never even knew I was trapped until I got broken free against my will into reality, the way my life was now meant chaos reigned; nevertheless I was now free.

I'm not sure if I enjoyed my freedom but it was certainly liberating to no longer be confined to a cell of my own making, I had no clue what was awaiting me anymore, tomorrow was now a mystery to me; a slightly unsettling thought. No plan, however, also meant no restrictions; all I could focus on was finding out more about the past.

Who was I really? Who was my family? What did my grandad look like? So many questions reigned supreme, so much so that I had new intentions of getting to the bottom of all that was unknown in my life. There was nothing I could do about it, for now, so I may as well let fun take over and see what tomorrow happens to bring.

Chapter Thirty-One

I woke up in my old room, for a brief moment (before reality had set in), I was happy; then all of what had happened over the last two months creeped in slowly. I put the pillow over my face and sighed.

"Morning Abz."

Juliette yawned as she greeted me, I pulled the pillow down then glanced at her.

"Morning Julz."

She wiped the sleep from her eyes as she continued to yawn.

"What's up Julz? You were quiet throughout our whole trip to Chicago, and on the way back."

She shrugged as I placed a worried look on my face.

"I'm fine, I just have a lot on my mind, your cousin was nice."

I threw the pillow that I was holding directly at her.

"Now I know something's wrong, how can you think she was *nice*? She is a lot of things but 'nice' is not one of them."

Juliette just threw the pillow back at me.

"Yeah she was a total cow, she was also the most beautiful girl that I have ever seen."

She peered off into the abyss of nothingness longingly.

I tried to set her straight.

"You gotta get over this obsession you have with looks Julz, it's not about what's going on outside. The thing that counts is what is going on with your insides. That girl is wicked through and through, I would much rather look like a one-eyed, lame duck while being a good person than be as pretty as her with that evil personality that she is sporting."

Juliette gawked at me in disbelief.

"Are you serious? You are telling me that you wouldn't trade a few of her features for a bit less of a moral compass?"

I matched her stern look.

"Yes Juliette that is exactly what I am saying! I have no interest in being beautiful, that just gets unwanted attention from dumb boys. I am happy as I am…"

Juliette turned away from me so I stopped talking briefly, I forget how upset she gets about these sorts of things.

"…as you should be too"

I finished my sentence after a long pause but she still didn't turn around to face me again.

Juliette replied with an annoyed edge to her voice.

"That's easy for you to say, you don't know what it's like to be ugly! Literally every female member of our family is stunning! Yet here I am, ugly and fat!"

She looked away from me and began staring into space.

"You're already so beautiful, just wait until you grow up. You'll be stunning just like the others."

She said this while talking to the wall, in an eerie tone of voice. She was seriously giving me the creeps.

"Only you think that of me Julz. If you asked all the boys at my old school they would all tell you I was their last choice. Besides I don't think you're ugly or fat."

I paused briefly waiting for a response. After all I received was silence I attempted some humour.

"I mean, I didn't like them either. What a bunch of 'Uggo's' right?"

Juliette finally faced me again and gave me a half-cocked attempt at a smile.

"That a girl."

I jested with her to get a real smile which in turn led her to poke her tongue out at me instead, so I returned the favour by sticking my tongue out in retaliation. I got my smile from her after that at least.

We got ready for the day, we both glammed up as today was the day we were going to meet with Patricia and company. I wanted us looking our best in order to rub it in their faces that I was doing great without her, who needed her poxy friendship? Looking good is definitely what we achieved, I didn't care what Cynthia or Patricia had to say, I knew we looked 'to die for' so they could shove those nasty comments where the sun doesn't shine.

My mum helped us by getting information as to where they might be hanging out today, she rang their parents who said that if I wanted to surprise them with a visit that I should head to Lake Clair Park. They were down at the lake again, apparently Cynthia was hosting a party there this time so that meant Patricia and her stupidly, perfect boyfriend Tyler were invited.

Once we had finally got down to the lake I was stopped from exiting the car, my legs had turned numb whilst the memory of last time poured into my mind, it felt as though a ten tonne weight was holding me down.

"What's wrong Abby?"

Juliette's voice had awoken me from my stasis.

"Huh? Oh, um... nothing. Is this really a good idea Julz? They smashed me into a million pieces last time I was here."

Juliette squeezed my hand tightly as I peered towards the group of kids gathering together.

Juliette spoke words of encouragement.

"You're not the same girl you were last time you were here, you are the strongest girl I know. You can do this Abz, you got this girl."

The last bit of her Speech just cracked me up, the way she tried to shorten my name even further while she changed her voice to sound all hip and American.

"Okay little miss hip-hop, *we* got this. I need you by my side or I am not going to get through this."

I shook off my remaining fear then stood out of the car fiercely; I advanced with purpose.

Nothing could stop me now, I walked over to where the group of kids were hanging out. I spotted Cynthia draping herself all over Tyler who was sitting next to Patricia, they were all laughing joyously until some boy came up and swept Cynthia to her feet. With that she was gone to mingle with the boy and some other kids, now was my chance to talk to Patricia and Tyler without Cynthia's involvement.

I snuck over to the table they were both sitting on unnoticed by the crowds, Juliette was following closely behind me. We sat down gently on the opposite side of the picnic bench, once we had sat down quietly we could hear their conversation.

"...I know Tyler, but she is a bit 'all over you'. You don't seem to do anything to deter her from sitting in your lap now *do* you?"

Patricia seemed upset about Cynthia's' flirtation towards Tyler, it was so unlike her, she was normally so secure in herself.

"Chill Babe, don't get all worked up over nothing, she is *your* friend. If you don't like it then go tell her yourself."

Tyler's words did not comfort her in the slightest.

"The fact you seem to enjoy her attention upsets me, not the fact that she is flirting with you. She

flirts with everyone, don't get a big head, I just wish you would stop encouraging her!"

Tyler kissed Patricia and reassured her on the fact that he loved her and not Cynthia.

I came to the conclusion that now was the time to intervene.

"Well, I wouldn't count your chickens Patz, Cynthia would betray her own mother to get what she wanted in life."

Shock covered Patricia's face.

"*Gail*, what the frick are you doing here *again*?"

Tyler's cheeks went bright red.

"Hey Gail, what brings you to our 'neck of the woods'?"

He was clearly nervous, I imagined him to be very guilty in regards to what he was being accused of. I continued with what I was saying.

"Cynthia was all over Tyler so I thought you might need support, you know the thing *good* friends do for each other."

My attention had now transferred over to Tyler while Patricia's mouth opened up as if she were trying to catch flies.

"Tyler, I am here on business, this is my associate Juliette."

Patricia scoffed.

"*Business*, what business could you and the piglet possibly have on your *agenda*?"

She gestured towards Juliette while saying the word piglet.

Anger took control of my face and mouth.

"HEY! Leave Juliette out of this *pint-size.*"

I rose from the table.

"The business that me and my cousin from England are doing in *your 'neck of the woods'*, as you put it Tyler, is the selling of our house. My mother thinks it is a good idea to say my goodbyes before we move to England."

Patricia stood to her feet in order to join me even though she only succeeded in reaching my chin by doing so.

"I don't know who you are anymore Abigail, you are *not* a friend of mine. I don't need a goodbye from you, thanks but no thanks."

I folded my arms tightly, I could see that Cynthia had noticed a commotion in our direction.

"Come on Julz, we're done here, I don't know why I bothered coming here when I so clearly didn't need to. Just so you know Juliette has been more of a friend to me over the last two months than

you have in the last two years. You don't know who I am? Try looking in a mirror, you might be able to recognise yourself but I certainly can't."

Juliette joined me in standing up whilst folding her arms just to copy me.

"Abby is the best person I know, you are a fool to choose *anyone* over her, let alone over a girl who clearly has her eyes set on *your* boyfriend."

With that we stormed off just in time so that we could avoid dealing with that witch Cynthia.

By the time we got to the car we could see a fuming Patricia telling Cynthia all about her encounter with me, I also saw Tyler grabbing Cynthia's bum while Patricia wasn't looking. Unfortunately for my ex best friend it appeared to be more than just an insinuation, I do believe Tyler and Cynthia were doing the dirty behind her back; it was now no longer my problem anymore.

"Drive, please."

I was in no mood for pleasantries.

"Sorry about her Julz, you're *not* a piglet."

Juliette laughed.

"Oh please Abby, I have been called far worse by much meaner girls before. You wait until you meet my fellow students."

I side hugged her while secretly hoping she was joking. As we drove back home again, I was really glad to be leaving Atlanta and heading back to England.

For the last few days we hung around and saw the local sites, Juliette and I had a great time while my parents met with real estate agents. I would miss our house even though it paled in comparison to my new English residence. Mum had found a buyer that was interested so it was just a matter of time before the sale went through.

At any rate, this was the last time I would stand in these pokey hallways, the last time I would bathe in the cupboard sized bathroom; sadly, it was also the last time I could sneak up into the attic to play. This house seemed so big when I was growing up, it felt like a castle to me, my memory didn't match the reality before me.

I remember running too fast down the laminated flooring which meant crash landing into my mother holding a basket of laundry sending her flying to the ground, she had looked like a ghost covered in all those white sheets. It was a sad moment while thinking back on all of the good times that made me pause, was this the right decision? Could we stay and pretend like the last three months had never actually happened? No, there was no going back to blissful ignorance, this was it.

You can't undo what has been done and you most certainly can't 'unknow' something either, the events of a mere twelve weeks of my life had rocked my entire being. It was amazing looking back at how innocent minded I truly was and yet this was just the tip of the iceberg, I dread to think what was around the corner.

There was a welcoming party of people as we were getting ready to embark on our new adventure, the neighbours were saying goodbye to my parents while I said goodbye to Milo. He was apologetic about ratting me out to my grandma, Juliette seemed terrified by his appearance so much so that I had to reassure her of the fact that he was indeed harmless.

The last of the shipping containers had been packed up which meant our house was bare, I had never seen it so empty before, this house was all I had known growing up. I had carved my name up into the attic walls however it had all been painted over now, it was as if we had never even lived there in the first place; it was as if the last fourteen years were just a dream.

It would soon be my fifteenth birthday and it would be the first one I wouldn't celebrate in this house, not that I felt like celebrating for *any* reason; my life was in shambles. There may be nothing left in this country for me but I was certainly going to miss it with every fibre in my being. Roll on England, let's see what disasters you will bring my way, I wonder if I will be strong enough to do what it takes to see my plan through.

Chapter Thirty-Two

Back in England all I could do is sleep (for nearly eight hours straight), my body clock was way off from all of that flying to and fro. When I woke up I firstly thought of checking out the recorded footage that should have been on my laptop, however there was only a few days worth of video. It was as if it had been wiped or maybe the internet went down, I wasn't going to jump to any conclusions just yet, there was only one video that contained any conversations.

Grandma Jean and Cliff were discussing her results that she had just received from the Doctor, there was a letter in her hand telling her that the experimental treatment had been unsuccessful, she was saying that she only had days to live; I had to tell my mother. Upon leaving my room I ran into Cliff, quite literally, I hit into him with full force which sent his tray of tea flying to the floor.

"Oh dear, I am *so* sorry Cliff."

I tried to help him pick up the broken pieces of teacup and biscuits but he was having none of it, he quietly sent me on my way; how does that man manage to never speak?

I raced to my mum's room and began knocking rapidly.

"Mum, are you in there?"

It was my dad that opened the door and let me in.

"What's going on Dad? Where's Mum?"

My dad had a solemn appearance.

"Your mum is by Grandma Jean's side, she is on her deathbed Abby, I'm sorry."

I fought back tears, why was I so sad about this cruel woman, maybe because if she dies the truth I so much needed would also die with her.

"Where are they?"

I felt my dad's clammy hand hold mine as he took me to the room that they were in.

"Oh Abby, just look at her, she looks so helpless."

My mother's tearful words rang true, Grandma Jean was hooked up to an IV drip and a heart monitor.

"Grandma Jean, it's me Abigail."

I gently touched her cold lifeless hand, she appeared to be so pale.

"I don't think she can hear you Abby."

We sat around in that room waiting for her to wake, but she never did.

In the middle of the night the heart monitor started going crazy, the nurses shooed us out of the room to try to save her but it was no good, she was gone. We had a funeral the very next day, we all said a few words about what she had meant to us but I chose not to do so. I didn't know what to say, I had barely known the woman, anything I did know about her I didn't like; I wasn't about to speak ill of the dead.

There was a lady dressed in black at the back of the Church, her face was covered with a veil so we couldn't see her face. I noticed mainly due to the fact that there was hardly anyone in the Church pews, I saw only the members of her household present apart from the veiled female, I hardly thought much of it at the time.

Once all of the Speeches were over that mysterious woman in black hobbled slowly down the aisle then got behind the pulpit, the weird thing I did notice was that the cane she was using to walk with was just like Grandma Jean's, she walked just like her too. That same eerie click could be heard, I was sure it was a 'W' carved into the wood.

They do say that grief can play tricks with your mind; that was probably what was happening. Maybe I was just being delusional, it was a very traumatic experience watching someone lose their life the way she did. As the unknown figure reached the pulpit she opened up the casket for us all to see, Grandma Jean wasn't in there; it was completely empty.

Chapter Thirty-Three

The auditorium filled with gasps, where was she? Had someone stolen her body? All of our questions were answered when the lady in black removed the covering away from her face, it was her, the vile woman had gone too far this time.

Grandma Jean was standing right in front of us fit and well, my mother stood up only to faint onto the ground. Her face was like snow as William stood up in outrage.

"YOU CRAZY WOMAN! What is wrong with you? Why would you do this to Deidre? To me? And all the rest of your family!?"

My father announced, outraged. I couldn't quite decide on how I should act but I did notice that Juliette's parents didn't seem as distressed as my mother and father. Could they have been in on it? Juliette just stared at me just as unsure as I was.

"Well now, I am just returning the favour to my faithless daughter William. Now she knows how it feels to have a loved one ripped away from her without so much as a goodbye!"

Jean replied snidely. Fury filled my father like he was a man possessed.

"She will have to go through all of this again when you actually do die, you cynical, devilish woman. What? Is it your dying wish to see her suffer?"

William retorted. Grandma Jean started laughing hysterically.

"My dear boy, I'm not dying! It was all a ruse to get you here, now that you have sold your house you are stuck with me. Truth be told I've always wanted to attend my own funeral. I guess I can mark that off my bucket list."

Her demeanour was maniacal at best, sadistic at worst. Her words were filled with venom.

My mother started to arouse.

"Mum is it really you? Am I dreaming Bill?"

My dad helped my mum to her feet.

"No Deidre, you are seeing things just how they are. Your mum has tricked us into coming to England just to make you suffer in a plot of revenge."

My mum started sobbing as she ran out of the Church, my dad followed closely behind her.

"So you found my security cameras and wiped them then?"

I said quietly. Grandma Jean smiled slyly towards where I was sitting.

"Of course you did. You cleverly left a video of you telling Cliff that you had only days to live so that I wouldn't question you."

Grandma Jean walked up to where I was sitting looking down at me with a wicked expression, simply beaming with glee at her ability to trick me.

"You should have known better than to try and trick a trickster. In my own home no less, nothing gets by me Abigail. I might be old but I'm sharp as a tac. It's not becoming to spy on people dear, this was simply tit for tat, I do hope you enjoy your stay at my estate. I am so terribly glad that you convinced your parents to move out here. It made my job so much easier. I can see you have my cunning but I've been in this game far longer than the likes of you. I may have underestimated you girl but I won't be making that mistake again."

I was so annoyed at myself for my part in her cruelty.

"So, was pretending to be dead just 'tit for tat' too?"

Without replying she walked out of the Church and into her limousine where Cliff drove her home, Juliette's family joined her which confirmed my suspicions. Maybe that's why they let Juliette come to Atlanta with me, they didn't want to risk her telling me what she was up to.

Back at the dwelling of my wicked grandmother I sat helpless blaming myself for everything. My mother was distraught; how could she do this to her? I know she felt betrayed by what she had done while pregnant with me but it didn't give her the right to torment my parents this way. The anger I felt fuelled my desire to get to the bottom of the secrets about our family, especially the ones that Grandma Jean were hiding.

She may be wise but I was a fast learner, it might take all that I had but I would get the best of that woman. I figured she was better as an ally than an enemy so I had to find a way to make her believe that I was on her side and not against her. I wasn't sure how I was going to do this but there had to be a way, she was always one step ahead of me.

That made me think, she might have had her own cameras hidden in my room, I searched up and down; I tore every inch of that room apart. I found no cameras but I did find a microphone, so that was how she was keeping tabs on all of us. I could use this to my advantage and trick her the way she tricked me, I could stage a conversation at the right time and lead her to believe that I was on her side.

Or would that be just what she was expecting? I wasn't sure if I should bring my parents into this, they had been through enough. Juliette had to be my only true friend in this situation. Well I hoped that she was genuinely my friend, more to the point I had little choice but to trust her at this stage, I had been burned by so many people in life recently.

I came to the conclusion that I had better be cautious in order to not reveal my plan to anyone, it was an isolating decision but it was best for everyone if I did this alone; I didn't want to risk anyone else getting burned by that Dragon woman. I couldn't involve Juliette while also trying to keep my cards close to my chest, for all I know Juliette told Grandma Jean about the cameras in the first place.

Chapter Thirty-Four

I began feeling the loneliness of my decision to move to this country, I was amongst strangers which still seemed preferable to my enemies awaiting me in America; every place I turned was another place that I didn't belong. Next week I had to go with Juliette to enrol in her all-girls boarding school, my mother had told me that I had no choice in the matter, in fact she had been awfully cold towards me ever since the revelation that my grandma was in fact alive.

I think she partially blamed me for deciding we should move here, it was my fault she had to move halfway across the world to avoid her mother and it was again my fault that she had returned to her clutches. There was no way out, no way of getting away from our fate, Grandma Jean had all the money and with it she had gained all of the control; we sold our house but it wouldn't be enough to start a life here.

In order to move out of Jean's prison we would first have to instigate a jailbreak, I feared we were not capable of escaping the fearsome wrath of Jean. They were out of work and had to join their mother's company in order to be able to live with Grandma Jean; she was not willing to let them live with her unless they were contributing in some way or another.

What had I done? Maybe it was really all my fault, my dad was sympathetic towards me but I sensed he too wasn't in the best of moods with me. He had lost his carefree demeanour that he had carried so well before, he started wearing drab coloured clothing and eating healthier.

I didn't recognise my parents anymore, they had become slaves to my grandmother's will, if she could fake her own death then she could literally do anything. It was time that I started gathering intel and fighting dirty, there was clearly no length this woman wasn't willing to go to in order to get what she wanted from people.

She had been in power for so long with no limits to her capabilities, money really did talk in this house, my mother had escaped from her once but there was no way that she was going to escape again. I needed to think big, I had to cut this dragon down at her legs so that we knew that she wouldn't be getting up again. I started to wonder what was most important to her, what did she care about the most? Was it staying in control? Was it money? Was it me?

I thought maybe she had orchestrated all of this so that she could be a part of my life, I wasn't sure if she cared for me at all anymore. I would have to find out her weaknesses and find out the route of what drives her, there had to be some goodness in her. I was going to find out anything and everything I could, there was a library full of varying literature, all sorts of different books to do with the history of this country and the history of the Mansion itself.

I figured there had to be information about my grandpa in there, his old study had been left untouched since his death or so I had heard, I would go investigate if it wasn't locked up tight; I would have to find a way in to see what secrets were hidden in there.

Firstly I would have to go uniform shopping with Juliette so my investigation would have to wait, Juliette was waiting for me in Cliff's car ready to take us to the shop. My mother had chosen not to join us so it was Christina my Aunty who was the one to take us instead.

"Hello Abigail, so gracious of you to join us."

Her tone was a little condescending to say the least.

"Sorry Aunty C, getting ready took longer than expected."

I sat in the car and did up my seatbelt while Christina eyed me up and down.

"No nicknames please, for me or my daughter, at least not in my presence and sit up straight!"

I straightened up slightly even though I had thought that I was straight enough already, there was little to no point in replying, anything I said would be shot down.

Aunt Christina was also not very pleased with me, she had recently found out that I had involved Juliette in deception by getting her to help me plant the cameras around the Mansion; good old Grandma Jean made sure she was made aware of it. There wasn't a low enough level in this world that the evil, fire-breathing, dragon woman wasn't willing to stoop to.

Once we had finally arrived at the uniform shop we were left alone to try on our school attire, oh how irritating the material felt against my skin. What had I done to these clothes to make them want to punish me? The material was rubbing against my neck while the rough collar felt as if it was strangling me; I'm not sure if it was the material or the tightness of the tie affixed inside of the material that made it unbearable.

"Juliette you can't seriously tell me that *this* is what I am expected to wear at your school."

I observed myself in the mirror, I looked like something out of a horror show. I had the appearance of the silly school girl character who is in the wrong place at the wrong time before she gets eaten alive by a werewolf.

The skirt went down to my knees which is where the socks reached, I had black dolly shoes on and a white shirt covered by an emerald blazer and matching tie.

"If I have to wear it then so do you, Abby."

I couldn't see her face but I could tell by the tone of her voice that she was enjoying my misery.

"Careful *Julz*, you don't want Mummy to hear us using nicknames."

I mocked her in return.

"Sorry about my mum, she is really upset with Dad at the moment."

Juliette seemed to be hurting.

I opened the changing room and joined Juliette as she left her stall, at least she looked just as ridiculous as I did.

"Are they still fighting then?"

Juliette sighed out loud as she inspected herself in the mirror.

"No it's much worse, they are now ignoring each other."

I sat down on the bench outside of the changing rooms.

"How is that *worse*?"

Juliette sat next to me.

"It means they have given up trying to resolve the problem, I am pretty sure a divorce is around the corner, they already asked to see a marriage counsellor and Dad has moved to the spare bedroom."

I placed my arm around her shoulders in an attempt to comfort her. Jeremy seemed like a stand up guy, I didn't think he was the problem, Christina however seemed to carry ice in her chest to replace the hole where her heart should be. Like mother like daughter in my opinion, she was definitely Jean's daughter, but I didn't know the full story yet.

Juliette reassured me that before the fighting began her mother was much more loving.

"So this is why you are taking so long than girls? Well I can see that the uniform fits you so hurry up and get them off so I can buy them, now."

The sound of Christina's sharp tone carried through me like an ice pick to a glacier.

"Yes, ma'am."

I saluted for effect as I headed off to the dressing room.

I was not looking forward to going to this school and wearing this ridiculous costume, It was only one year (or so I kept telling myself), soon I would be out of school seeing as it was England and school finished at a younger age here. I just hoped that the people were friendlier in this country, or at least less stuck-up, anything had to be better than enduring people like Heather, Patricia and Cynthia(**UGH**).

Chapter Thirty-Five

The first day of school had arrived, I was dressed in my uniform like a good little girl hating every minute of it, Juliette was in the year below me at school so she would not be joining me in my classes unfortunately.

Cliff was the one to take me to meet my Headmaster as my parents were 'too busy with work', an extremely lame excuse if you ask me. I was beginning to get extremely annoyed with their petty reasons for not being around me, I didn't fake my own death like some other people in our family yet I got the brunt of their annoyance.

To be fair, they weren't speaking to my grandmother either, or each other much, the separate room factor had been a problem for their relationship. At night they would sneak into each other's room but they would slink back out first thing in the morning, however lately they had been spending less nights together than before.

My room wasn't far away so I could hear the doors when they opened and closed, so I knew when they were visiting each other, In time I'm sure things would get back to normal. I forgave them for their secrets and lies so you would think that they would forgive me for my slight error in judgement, unless Grandma Jean was the cause of their behaviour.

I wouldn't put it past her, she has had it in for my parents ever since they were just kids. The Headmaster was very old, he looked like he was seconds away from becoming a skeleton, he appeared to be so frail as he pitter-pattered over to his chair.

"You must be Miss Abigail Wilson, pleasure to meet you, any relative of Miss Jean Winterberry (this was her maiden name before she married) is welcome here."

Her married name was Williamson which my parents legally changed to Wilson when they got to America in order to cover their tracks.

All the good it did them as Grandma Jean still found them in the end, this man clearly knew my grandma from before she married.

"Jean was one of our best students here at Cobham Hall."

He leant forward and passed me a black and white picture of Jean in her uniform, behind it was a picture of my mother in that very same uniform years later. They looked so similar to each other in those pictures.

"Thank You, sir."

I handed the pictures back to his shaking hand.

"Call me Mr Henderson young miss."

The folds of his skin that covered his eyelids made his eyes appear to be nearly closed when he smiled.

A grin which consisted of four teeth in total (yes, I counted).

"OK, Thank You, Mr Henderson."

He stood up shakily from his chair and extended his hand, as terrifying as it was to hold a near-dead man's hand I knew I had to. I stood up and shook his hand very slowly so as not to break any bones.

"Welcome to Cobham Hall, Miss Jensen will show you to your class."

A much younger lady was being pointed at, she could now take me out to the classrooms, at this stage Cliff had left me to it and went on his way.

"Pleasure to meet you Miss Abigail, your teacher will be Mrs Henderson."

I gawked at her terrified, expecting a little old lady to be my teacher.

"I know what you're thinking."

I really didn't think she did.

"Mrs Henderson is the wife of Mr Henderson's grandson."

Fear left my face as I realised a nice healthy young person (someone who wouldn't be dying any time soon) would be in charge of my learning in the last year of school.

"Oh, okay... cool."

I said, trying to act like I hadn't been fearing the worst. Miss Jensen knocked on the door and guided me in.

The young teacher greeted us cheerfully.

"Hello Mrs Henderson, this is Abigail Wilson and she will be joining your class for the year."

I glanced around at the blank faces of the class.

"Hi."

I waved just a little.

"Welcome Abigail, is that your preferred name?"

Mrs Henderson was nothing like her grandfather (which was good), she was nowhere near death's door.

"Abby is fine."

I blushed just a bit, it was so awkward facing those intrigued faces and hushed tones, I knew the second that they heard my accent they would know I wasn't English.

"Okay Abby, take a seat next to Sabrina Blackwell."

She gestured to an empty seat in the front row of the class.

Oh how I hated being in the front row.

"That'll be all, Miss Jensen."

With that she scurried out of the door, leaving me alone in a pit of sleeping lions, I sat down praying she wouldn't ask me any awkward questions.

"There are three rules in this class Abby, I cannot abide tardiness, speaking out of turn or incessant chatter. If you can cope with that, you and I will get along just fine."

I nodded as I peered down at the book in front of me, it was like a foreign language to me. Sabrina didn't say much to me and definitely did not try to befriend me, Mrs Henderson was very strict but seemed to be a good teacher.

Lunch time couldn't come fast enough, I searched everywhere for Juliette, I eventually found her in the lunchroom eating on a table all by herself. The dinner lady served me what I think was food, let's just hope it tastes better than it looks; I had a green lump of jello, a slosh of sludgy mash and a scoop of what I was hoping to be normal meat in watery gravy.

Juliette waved me over to her table where I sat down immediately as soon as I got to her.

"This place is a nightmare Julz. The teachers won't let me listen to my music in class, even when we're writing in our books, and this food…"

I trailed off while staring at my food as if it was a foreign contaminant.

Juliette couldn't help but laugh almost hysterically at me.

"Come on Abz, it tastes better than it looks."

I gaped at her in disbelief while I tried a bite, I immediately spat it back into my napkin.

"Shall I add 'being a liar' to your resume Julz?"

I raised my eyebrows to the roof as Juliette continued giggling, she soon went eerily quiet mid-laugh.

"Who's your *friend,* Drooliette?"

Juliette's expression was infinite horror as I turned to face who was the cause behind her being so afraid. When I turned around I saw Sabrina Blackwell standing behind another girl who was the size of a house.

I think she may have eaten her own family in order to gain that much weight, she quite literally couldn't be more gruesome if she tried. Her face looked as if it had been stung by a bumble bee which had in turn caused her whole body to swell up from anaphylactic shock.

"Hi, my name is Abby, I am Juliette's cousin. It's a pleasure to meet you."

I held out my hand in order to greet the monster, secretly hoping she didn't bite me.

"Well *Shabby*, welcome to *my* school. Stay out of my way and I will stay out of yours, got it?"

With that she folded those pudgy arms of hers then practically growled at me. It was apparent to me that she owned 'the joint' and we were expected to follow her rules.

I wasn't about to challenge her being the size she was, she could literally sit on me and I would get lost up her butt cheeks. Her skills seemed to consist of eating everything, giving out really bad nicknames and growing hair in places there shouldn't be any hair at all (for women at least). Maybe she was part human, part bear, all I knew was that the plump hairy beast made the decision to leave and I was glad to see the back of them; for now.

Sabrina and the oversized miss piggy trotted off back to whence they came, hopefully never to return.

"Who was that Julz?"

Juliette spoke in hushed tones, as if her spies could be anywhere and everywhere.

"Wilma Renforth."

That's all she gave me, just a name.

"Should that name mean something to me somehow?"

Juliette would not stop looking over her shoulder.

"She basically owns the school, everyone is afraid of her and she only leaves me alone because my family is rich but she enjoys bullying anyone she feels like with very little cause."

I inspected the cafeteria becoming puzzled.

She had disappeared as quickly as she appeared, despite her size she moved fast.

"Is it just because she is big or does her family have some sort of power?"

Juliette shrugged her shoulders, she either didn't know or didn't want me to know, whatever the reason I wasn't getting any more information out of her.

I felt out of my depth with this school, with scary bullies and strict teachers, even the lunch room was spookily silent. We couldn't use our phones or mp3 players on the school grounds and the school work was all new to me.

I witnessed the school bully stealing lunch money, pinning kids against lockers and punching students in the arm as they walked by her in the hall. Juliette was right with what she had said to me, we were not her target. Sabrina seemed a sideline act nevertheless she definitely played her part in terrifying the pupils.

Once at home Juliette felt it was safe to tell me Wilma's story, her parents owned a shell corporation so had money but no time for their daughter. She had a genetic condition which was why she became so big, the parents tried everything to get her to diet but it was no good the girl never felt full and was obsessed with food. It was like a drug to her, she had a lot of health conditions, they operated on her to make her stomach smaller with a gastric band. She had apparently lost a stone of weight since the operation last year.

Since then she became angry at not being able to eat what she wanted (without her stomach exploding), her new obsession was making others as miserable as she was. Her stooge Sabrina was her best friend growing up and had chosen to follow her dark path for her own selfish reasons, amongst them was her own safety. She had tried to confront Wilma once before and earned a harsh slap across her face, Sabrina never wanted to challenge her ever again.

Chapter Thirty-Six

The school decided that it was a good idea to give Juliette and I an assignment for extra credit, we had to develop something together that represents our family and what it means to us. I had the perfect idea of a family tree and an essay which Juliette also agreed to, it meant I had an excuse to rummage through the family archives and find out all about my family members.

When we got home that night I spoke with Grandma Jean and she was more than happy to help us out with names and dates of the members in her side of the family, Dad helped me with the rest of the information about his family members.

Dad's parents (both now deceased) Elaine Chesterfield/Spencer (Mum) Maurice Spencer (Dad)	Mum's parents (Father now deceased) Jean Winterberry (Mum) Derek Williamson (Dad)
Dad's Sister (Aunty) Angela Miller/Spencer **Dad's sister's Husband (uncle)** Robert Miller	Mum's Sister (Aunty) Christina Williamson/Robinson **Mum Sister's Husband (Uncle)** Jeremy Robinson
Dad (surname legally changed) William Spencer (now Wilson)	Mum (surname legally changed) Deidre Williamson (now Wilson)
Dad's Niece (Cousin) Heather Miller	Mum's Niece (Cousin) Juliette Robinson
Me (Daughter) Abigail Wilson	Me (Daughter) Abigail Wilson

That was what I had so far, Juliette had her own version from her perspective as well, I had yet to show it to all members of the family; I left a blank space in case there were some missing people on there we need to add. It was looking good, although I missed the part of how my dad was also my mum's adopted brother, I figured that it was okay to leave that part out.

Juliette had an extra section on her family tree that even I didn't know about. Who was Simon Robinson-Green? I wanted to ask her but I was worried she might get upset with me. I tried to ask in a playful way.

"Hey, shall I add Simon onto my chart? I got some space left."

Juliette just shook her head.

I guess that meant she was not going to talk about it with me. We spent all week working on our essays about our family; I completed my research by reading every book we had about our family's heritage. We were descendants from wealthy landowners dating way back to the eighteen-hundreds, my dad's family were farmers originally from England but more than a hundred years ago they emigrated to America for a better life; William's grandfather found wealth and passed it onto his descendants.

My grandfathers on both side were business partners, soon after they all became friends. I had no idea who would have wanted my grandparents dead so I had to assume the helicopter accident was just that, an accident. It seemed to me that the only person who had something to gain from the helicopter accident would be Grandma Jean but why would she want her husband dead?

The helicopter incident was marked as an accident due to the fact that they couldn't find proof that it was maliciously destroyed, but forensics weren't as good back then. Without any reason to be, I was suspicious of Grandma Jean, how was she the last one standing out of the grandparents?

Mum and dad seemed pleased with my work and enjoyed my essay, Juliette's parents weren't as thrilled with her presentation.

"Why did you include *Simon* in your family tree?"

Juliette's mum was complaining whilst she was sulking.

"He is *my* brother isn't he?"

Jeremy sat, head in his hands, refusing to even acknowledge the conversation.

"You haven't even met him so he hardly deserves a spot on the family tree now does he?"

Her mother was adamant.

"Who's fault is that?"

Juliette stomped her feet as she spoke like a teeny toddler.

"I have been asking to meet him ever since you told me about him"

Christina was having none of it.

"I don't wish to discuss this with you now or ever, so drop it!"

Juliette sat back down and continued sulking into her soup.

"She has a point Christina."

Jeremy finally made the choice to say something, although it only fuelled the fire under Christina making her even angrier than before.

"We will talk about this in couples counselling."

With that they both backed down and left it alone.

So Juliette had a brother, I assume it was from before he married Christina, if not that might explain why they were having such problems. Did he cheat on Christina? No wonder she seems so angry all of the time. I wanted to ask Juliette about it but I also didn't want to push her before she was ready, I had enough of my own drama to worry about at the moment.

This family just got more and more complex, the deeper I got into the murky waters the more I felt I may drown. The worst part was that I didn't have a friend in the world to confide in, I had all this anguish and anxiety locked up inside with no way to release it. I missed Patricia as much as I was mad at her, we had been friends for such a long time. Did anger cloud my judgement?

I left her with that evil witch with her talons so deeply rooted into Tyler. I thought of different ways to reach her, maybe I could crawl along on my belly begging for forgiveness like I had done in the past. Would she even listen to me?

I would talk to Juliette but she has enough going on, as much as I wanted to know what the deal was when it came to her brother Simon I wasn't about to involve myself in a family feud. I'm sure, in time, she would let me know or my parents would. It was my birthday next week so they had chosen to have a family dinner (like we don't do that every day already).

I could not wait to be fifteen, maybe then I would get a bit more freedom, I am virtually a grown up already. It was about time they all started treating me a bit more grown up, I wanted to get into my granddad's old study and also visit the family company.

The more I knew the better chance I had of finding out what Grandma Jean's weakness was and how to take her down. The family tree was just the beginning, I needed more information about this family one way or another.

Chapter Thirty-Seven

It was finally a day of celebration when October nineteenth had decided to arrive and with it my fifteenth birthday was here, upon waking up I noticed something different about my room... PRESENTS!

Someone must have snuck into my room while I was asleep in order to put them there (a little bit creepy), In a rush to open them I forgot to check who they were from, there were so many boxes covered in sparkly silver wrapping paper wrapped in pastel pink ribbons tied into bows.

There were fifteen presents in total one for every year of my life, the biggest one was filled to the brim with packing peanuts, I sifted through the entire box in order to find a present but to no avail. I opened them each in turn going from largest to smallest, small pebbles were in one, shells in another, it was bizarre I couldn't quite figure out the meaning behind it all. Once I had reached the tiniest of all the presents a note was inside of it, however when I picked up the note a small key fell out of it, the note read as follows:

Clues to a birthday puzzle surprise, I hope you will enjoy figuring it all out

P.S. come to the green room when you have the answer

That was all, how strange. I looked again at the contents of each box, fifteen things in total and I resolved to write a list in order from largest to smallest:

1. Packing peanuts
2. Shells
3. Sand
4. Ice lolly sticks
5. Pebbles
6. Straws
7. Empty coconut shells
8. Dried seaweed
9. Palm leaves
10. A travel magazine
11. An empty photo album
12. A single use camera
13. A tin of crab meat
14. A locked box

15. A small key (and a note)

There seemed to be a tropical theme alongside a sense of travel so maybe my present was a holiday. Grandma Jean had to be behind this, who else could have orchestrated this whole 'presents full of clues' idea. Upon further inspection the tiny key seemed to fit the lock of the box from present number fourteen, I twisted the miniature key until the locked box clicked and was now open. Inside was a picture of a young girl on the beach in a hula grass skirt making a sandcastle, I turned over the old photo and on the back it read:

Deidre age 8

Holiday in Hawaii

It was my mother on holiday and the writing on the back of the photo matched the writing of the note perfectly. I assume that means I am going to Hawaii with my mother or possibly the whole family, I was going to have to go to the green room if I was going to find out for sure; so that is just what I did.

There was a trail of paper decorative flowers leading the way and a sign greeting me above the door into the green room, it read **HAPPY 15th BIRTHDAY ABBY**. I had to admit this had to be the most fuss I had ever received over any birthday of mine in the past; I was without a doubt enjoying the attention. It was welcoming to have a distraction to take my mind off all of the dark secrets that plagued my family, I opened the door so slowly, a creak could be heard as I entered the room.

It was pitch black so I turned on the light and as I did I saw my entire family jump out as if from nowhere and shout.

"HAPPY BIRTHDAY!"

They popped party string and blew birthday trumpets, for the first time since arriving in England I felt a little less alone in the world. I peered around the room full of these oddballs that were my family, I grew up with just my parents for over fourteen years but now I had a real family.

They had their issues but it was lovely to know they cared about me, after the shock wore off I shed tears of joy as my mother squeezed the life out of me.

"We're proud of you kiddo, you are becoming a beautiful woman right before my very eyes."

My dad always knew just what to say to put a smile on my face.

"Thanks Dad, thanks everyone."

Grandma Jean stood in front of me while everyone else moved aside to make room for her.

"So Abby, tell me, did you like your presents?"

I grinned at her. When I imagined having a Grandma, I could never have guessed that this conniving woman in front of me would be it.

"Yes Grandma, are we flying to Hawaii?"

This sly smile spread across my grandma's face. I knew if I played her game I would eventually find a way to get one up on her.

"Well done, I knew you would figure it out, I want to take you to your mother's favourite holiday destination when she was a child."

I was thrilled to visit such an exotic country but there was a feeling of dread that I just couldn't escape deep inside of me.

"Did you take my mother there with Grandad?"

My grandmother's face changed at the sound of that word 'Grandad,' she had a deep sadness escaping from inside her like I had never seen before. I had clearly caught her off guard.

"He would have loved to hear you call him that."

Her dissatisfied half smile made me doubt her involvement in the helicopter accident, maybe she wasn't to blame or maybe she just felt sorrow over what she had done.

It was difficult to judge the situation but for now I settled to enjoy my birthday and the time with my family, I could always worry about finding out the truth when we were back. I hugged my grandma which ultimately left her Speechless, this woman acted as if she knew no love but I was determined to show her some anyway. She patted the back of my head briefly and then pulled away seemingly uncomfortable with the affection I was lavishing upon her.

"Best gift ever."

I whispered as she left my arms, I was determined to play the part of 'most grateful granddaughter' to date.

"Thank you everyone, I look forward to celebrating my birthday with all of you in HAWAII!"

I shrieked with excitement and ran off to pack.

Hawaii was amazing; there was a large luxurious beach cabin with staff to take care of us. I wouldn't expect anything less where my grandma was concerned, the beach was endless with its white hot sand and green blue waves crashing onto it; making it utterly picturesque.

There was a boy sitting on the sand in the distance, his olive skinned glowed in the sunshine, I saw Juliette out of the corner of my eye run up to greet him shouting 'SIMON!' at the top of her lungs. So this was the mysterious Simon I kept hearing about. Everyone was so cloak and dagger about who he was, I was curious to see what all the fuss was about. He jumped out of the sand brushing himself off and embraced her on sight, they were talking excitedly but I couldn't hear what they were saying to each other.

I glanced in the direction of Christina and Jeremy only to see Christina's stern stance with arms folded glaring at them while Jeremy seemed happier than I had ever seen him before. Jeremy started waving at the two of them and gestured for them to come closer. Simon was like something out of an action movie, his muscle covered body glistened while his chiseled jawline could cut glass.

He had adorable dimples when he smiled which made him look even more handsome, his slicked-back hair the colour of coal was like something out of a magazine. How did this boy fit into *our* family? As he came closer to where we were I felt my heart racing a mile a minute.

"Son, how good to see you again! I'm so glad your mother let you come."

Jeremy's words hit me like a ton of bricks, how was *this* guy his son? I know I suspected as much but the fact I was right surprised me, along with the fact that his son looked like a model.

He had to be about seventeen or so, according to my calculations, although to me he appeared to be older than he was supposed to be. Simon and Jeremy had a touching embrace while Christina seemed to be highly unamused.

"Hello Father... Mother, she is also here with me."

He had an accent that I couldn't quite recognise however he spoke English very well.

"Just perfect Jeremy, now your mistress and the child you share with her will be joining us on our family holiday, are you happy now?"

Jeremy ignored Christina's statement of unhappiness over the situation and took Simon into the beach cabin.

Christina stormed off to the bar that was set up outside on the beach. It seemed my existence had not even been acknowledged as I sat there drooling over the new boy, I now knew that Jeremy had cheated on Christina but there had to be more to the story.

Simon was much older than Juliette and he must have had him first, I was desperate to know what was going on.

"Julz, come here."

I whispered loudly as she headed in my direction.

"What's up Abz?"

She seemed so casual about the whole thing.

"Are you going to tell me what on earth is going on?"

Juliette glanced around to see if anyone was listening in.

"Okay, but you have to keep it to yourself."

Her regard was stern before moving further afield. She walked far away from the cabin.

"Simon is my brother, my father had an affair with our maid before I was born."

I stroked her arm sympathetically.

"Sorry Julz."

I didn't really know what to say but I did feel bad for her situation

My silence just stirred Juliette on.

"It's okay Abz, my mum was a workaholic and refused to start a family so my dad became lonely. He didn't know about Simon, my mum found out about the affair and fired our maid then she was never heard from again, or so my dad thought. My mum was the one who found out about Simon and hid him from my dad for years, she was sending cheques for his upkeep and to silence her. That is why they keep fighting, I invited Simon here to Hawaii as we have been writing in secret."

It was worse than I had first thought.

"So your mum will be pretty upset to see Simon's mum again, then?"

Juliette sighed loudly.

"Yes I can imagine so, but I had no choice, she was refusing to let me see my own *brother*."

Her face had a pained expression.

"I get it, I'm sure your mum will calm down, eventually."

With that conversation over, we headed back to the cabin to enjoy my birthday celebrations.

I couldn't get over what a hunk Simon was, he was tall like his father but covered head to toe in muscles, there was a stunning woman standing next to him, she certainly didn't look like a maid. Her hair mirrored Simon's however hers was long and flowed down her back, she had a beautiful flower in her hair pinning one side of it behind her ear, she looked as if she belonged here in Hawaii.

The lady shared the same accent as her son and spoke English just as well, her laughter filled the entire room and she had such warmth to her presence. She was Slim but had womanly curves that would drive any man crazy.

Upon listening to the conversations around me I discovered they both lived here in Hawaii and Simon's mother's name was Miriam. Miriam had originally worked for Grandma Jean and Grandpa in the Hawaii beach cabin but she had come to the UK to study so Grandma Jean offered her a job in the Mansion while she was here.

Unfortunately Jeremy took a shine to her and one thing led to another, Simon seemed to be very okay with where he came from and spoke proudly about his mother. As I gazed longingly at Simon he remained completely unaware of my existence, I wanted to talk to him but every time a thought entered my head my mouth turned into sandpaper.

It was a good birthday, the best I had ever had, we spent most of the school holidays in Hawaii and we had lots of delicious local delicacies to sample. I got to speak to Simon briefly as we were saying goodbye, his words were **'Goodbye Abigail, I'm hoping you enjoy your birthday here in Hawaii.'** while I said **'Thanks.'** quietly and grinned like a Cheshire cat.

Jeremy embraced both mother and son before getting on the plane while Christina was already on the plane breaking into the liquor cabinet. It didn't look good for Juliette's parents, they were talking less and less while Christina just drank more and more, Juliette was just so happy to spend time with her brother however she seemed not to care about the distress her mum was in.

Now it was back to reality, it was so delightful to have those two days in paradise, it helped me forget about all the drama back home; unfortunately with the plane ride home everything returned back to normal.

As normal as this dysfunctional family could be at any rate, Cliff had not joined us on the trip which was unusual but nearly unnoticeable. He literally never spoke, the only way you could know if he was approaching is by the sound of his keys jangling as he walked.

He kept a key to every door in the house which didn't half make a racket as he walked around the place, if he had every key that would mean he had to have a key to Grandpa's sealed old study. How would I be able to get his keys? Even more importantly, how would I know which key opens that door? I would have to spy on Cliff or acquire his keys somehow, however, that was a problem for another day; right now I am going to enjoy the ride home.

Chapter Thirty-Eight

Two months had been and gone, I had been watching Cliff without his knowledge and had been monitoring the likely location of where my grandpa's study was. There was a sealed room which no one went into however I had seen Cliff on occasion enter the room, he only ever entered it briefly which meant I was right in thinking he was the one with the key to open it.

It was nearly Christmas so that meant Cliff was due to take his yearly holiday abroad, I had been gathering intel on him by speaking to other members of staff, there was a spare set of keys that was used only in emergencies or when Cliff was on holiday.

I had already snuck out the spare set of keys for a test drive however much to my despair there was one vital key missing from the set, the one key that I needed. I had thought of an idea on how to copy the key but the key was old and apparently irreplaceable, the lock also was pretty sturdy and I haven't so far been able to break into the room. My only choice left was to get Cliff away from his keys but he slept with them attached to his person, I had nearly given up all hope until one night things changed for the better.

I had been struggling to sleep so I got up to grab a glass of milk to help me settle down into a deep slumber, when I had nearly reached my room I was startled by the movement of a figure in the hallway close to where I was standing. I crept up and hid behind a marble statue as I saw Cliff, he couldn't be wearing his keys because he wasn't making a sound.

He left the house in such a hurry and drove off into the night, I quietly entered his room and saw his set of keys on the nightstand. In his rush to leave he must have left them behind either that or he needed them off in order to leave the house stealthily. I saw this as my one and only chance to get into that secret room no one wanted me to get into, I removed the key that I needed and left the keys nearly exactly as I had found them.

This was it, I had gained access to this mysterious room where my grandpa spent next to all his time in, I was shaking from head to toe with terror and thrill spreading to every part of my body. I put the key into the lock and turned it, as I did it felt as though I could hear my own heartbeat as loud as the sound of a drum banging in my ears, with the last turn of the key the heavy door started to move forward.

I had my cell phone with me so I could take pictures of anything suspicious that I may find. The plan was to get in and get out as quickly as possible, I took pictures of any documents that appeared to be important. Looking around curiosity got the better of me, I had expected for the room to be dusty and untouched as my grandma had said no one had entered it since the death of her husband, a fact I knew was untrue but still expected it to look less used.

Cliff must be using it for his own personal private office, he had records for everything dating back years since before I was born. I photographed everything that I could then put it back just as I found it. I wanted to find more than just financial records. I was hoping to find pictures of Grandpa or something of his that I could use in order to get to know more about him. I took a gander at the bookshelf, it was filled with books of every kind.

I noticed there were encyclopaedias up on a high shelf, on first glance they appeared to be normal apart from one book; the date was wrong on the spine of one of the books. I had to get the attached sliding ladder in order to reach it, I just wanted to take a closer look to see why the date was wrong but as I pulled the book I began to feel a movement. The bookcase was moving with me on it! What on earth had I gotten myself into?

Everywhere I turned there was only darkness that could be seen, I was utterly petrified, could there be monsters hiding in my grandpa's bookcase? Why did he have a secret door and where did it lead? I couldn't turn back now, not when I had come so far, I just had to find out what was in here with me so I turned on my torch mode which was on my mobile phone; it was such a surprise what I saw next. Thankfully nothing scary was in here with me, definitely no monsters lurking unless you count the hundreds of spiders that it must have taken to create all the cobwebs that were covering the hidden room.

I saw a lantern with a box of matches next to it which meant I could use the matches to light the old lantern, I was now in my grandpa's study. I thought the first room was where he did all his work but it turns out that he had his study here behind the bookcase all along. There was a desk with a lamp on it and a photo of him and Grandma when they were younger, Grandma looked happy in a way I had never witnessed myself whilst Grandpa's appearance was so handsome.

Such joy filled my heart because I was finally seeing the face of my grandpa for the first time, he appeared to be such a kind man. Happiness turned to sorrow as I thought of the reason why I had never seen his face before now, even Cliff must not know about this place or it wouldn't be completely untouched since my grandpa's death. I knew I would find what I needed from this room. I opened the top draw of his noble desk, it was an emerald coloured desk fit for a king with gold detailing covering the legs and draw doorknobs.

There was a diary in the draw that belonged to my grandpa and in it were his thoughts and feelings. As I flipped through the pages to his last entry, a letter fell out. It had the words *'To whomever shall find this* letter, in the event of my death please give this to my beloved wife.'. It read as follows:

I am concerned for my own safety, I warned you not to come with me on my business trip tomorrow, I don't want anything happening to my beloved. I made the mistake of trusting the wrong person, I just wish I knew who that person was. We had a fight again last night as I'm sure you still think I am sleeping with Elaine. Why would you think I would do such a thing? You should know that I love you deeply. You brought me my daughters whom I love unconditionally. If anyone is reading this who is not my wife and I am not alive, please call the police, there is no way that my death was an accident.

I have been collecting evidence and have found out that someone is stealing from my company, it has to be someone who works for me and has gained my trust. I have one main suspect in mind and when I get back from my business trip I will be sure to reveal this trickster, I am only awaiting confirmation from my bank. My only wish is that I spend less time working and more time with my family, in my study is my only freedom from the stress I have been under.

When I get back from this trip I will leave the company in the care of the board while I take some much needed time off, I just need this deal to go through. If these are my last words then let it be said that Jean is the love of my life and I trust her with every fibre of my being, Jean you are the love of my life and you always will be. You are the reason I *fought so hard to make my business a success, I know you hated me working such long hours but everything will change when I get back, I promise.*

Forever yours, your husband.

Derek Williamson

Tears filled my eyes and I knew what I had to do, I had my doubts about Grandma but if my grandpa trusted her I was going to as well.

Chapter Thirty-Nine

I raced out of the secret room and locked the study behind holding the diary tightly under my arm, Grandma Jean was fast asleep but this couldn't wait.

"Grandma, wake up, please."

I shook her as I spoke.

"Abigail what is the meaning of this? What time is it?"

She was startled and angry but I had to show her what I had managed to find.

"I found Grandpa's diary, inside was a letter and you have to read it!"

She turned on her bedside table lamp and grabbed her reading glasses.

"Where did you find this?"

I opened the page of his last entry, as she began reading she looked as if she had seen a ghost.

"I found Grandpa's secret study, it was behind the bookcase."

A solitary tear rolled out of my grandmother's left eye, I had never seen her vulnerable like this before.

"Show me, please Abby, take me there."

It was nice hearing her call me Abby again, but now wasn't the time to comment on it. I helped her out of her bed and we went to the study. I opened it up and showed her how I got into the secret room.

She ebbed slowly towards the desk where her husband had been secretly visiting nights on end while she fed and bathed the kids, as she sat down in his chair she saw the picture he kept on his desk.

"This was our last holiday in Hawaii together, I can't believe he kept this picture on his desk."

She picked it up and kissed the face of her now deceased husband in the picture.

"Do you think the helicopter accident was actually done on purpose?"

She placed the picture back down as she shrugged her shoulders, she seemed to be entranced by the room we were in.

"I have photos of Cliff's records, he uses the other side of the room we were just in, I have seen him coming and going from here. I noticed something odd from the records in his desk."

I showed her a transaction that was recorded around the time of the helicopter accident, it was a large sum of money that Cliff had sent to a man by the name of Trent Mcphee.

"He has also been sending money to an offshore account each month since before Grandpa died."

Grandma Jean woke up from her spell as she grabbed my phone then peered at the pictures I had taken.

"I know this name, Trent Mcphee, he was questioned after your grandpa died. He was the one who signed off on the safety check of the helicopter that your grandpa was in when he died."

She paused as the unthinkable entered her head.

"How could I have been so blind, Cliff! Of course it was Cliff, all this time I trusted that he was on *my* side. He was the one who convinced me that your grandpa was cheating on me, he filled my mind with stories of how I deserved better; he was the one friend I thought I had in this world. It can't be, he couldn't do this to me surely, could he do this to me?"

My grandmother stumbled to find the words to express the unthinkable truth that was befalling; there was no other explanation.

Chapter Forty

Cliff was behind everything, his silent evil had infiltrated this house as he pitted my grandparents against each other and gained the trust of both of them. He had been the one stealing the funds from Grandpa and the bank was going to reveal him as the culprit so Cliff paid someone off to get rid of him, my dad's parents were just collateral damage.

"I thought he was just an old fool but he saved my life, I had believed he wanted to be around Elaine without me but he just wanted me to be safe."

Floods of tears fell from her eyes as if the anger she had been holding onto all of these years had been their barrier and now they were free.

Sorrow could be heard in Grandma Jean's voice as she spoke.

"The last words he ever said to me were 'I love you' and mine were 'have fun with Elaine' as I slammed the door in his face."

Regret filled her voice as she looked completely drained from life.

"Where is Cliff Abby?"

I gaped at her without knowing what to say, the void inside her was too great to be filled.

"I saw him leave in a hurry, he took his private car and drove off."

I was becoming a little flustered.

"Up to no good I'm sure of it, are you sure this is the only key to this room?"

I nodded slowly.

"I have checked and this is the only set of keys, he left his keys on his bedside table."

With that Grandma Jean sent me to bed and told me she would deal with everything. If I could do it all over again I would have stayed with her, instead all I did was hesitate before retiring to my bedroom.

I couldn't sleep, all I could do was pace up and down, back and forth, what was I thinking leaving my frail old Grandma to deal with the evil Cliff? All this time I thought that *she* was the mastermind behind all of the bad happening in my life, it was *Cliff.*

Cliff had also helped my parents flee to America because he wanted them out of the way (I assume), I saw on his bank records that he had transferred money to my mother's account just before she would have left to go live in America. He killed three of my grandparents, if that wasn't enough he had then fooled the other grandparent of mine into believing that he was the only one on her side.

I heard the front door close then there were speedy footsteps in the hallway, I had ended up deciding that I needed to be by my grandma's side so I snuck out and round to my grandma's bedroom. I could hear voices.

"Cliff the game is up, I know about *everything*."

It was my grandma's voice that I heard first.

"You killed my husband Cliff, the least you could do is tell me, why?"

Cliff's voice sounded just like his personality, it was the first time that I was hearing it but if snakes could talk that is how they would sound.

"I did it for *us* Jean, your husband didn't deserve you, he was cheating on you."

The venomous sound sent shivers down my spine.

"I know that is a lie Cliff, I found his journal."

Grandma was not backing down, she had been taken for a fool for way too long.

"Why did you take him away from me? The truth Cliff!"

He knew he had no way out of this one.

His lies weren't going to work on her anymore.

"Fine, I will tell you the truth you stupid old fool, your husband was inches away from finding out that I was the one stealing from his business accounts. I intercepted a call from the bank while he was preparing for his business trip, it was while you two were fighting about Elaine."

He laughed wickedly as the fight had been his doing.

"You venomous snake, you've been twisting my thoughts all this time! Manipulating me like your own personal doll! How could I have been so blind to your dastardly endeavours!"

Jean protested but it only served to spur Cliff on.

"I had convinced you that Elaine had her claws into your husband so it wasn't hard to get you two to lock horns, the bank informed me that they had the information on the unauthorised user of the business accounts. It wouldn't be long until he would contact the bank himself as to why they hadn't called, so I paid a man off to forge a report to say the helicopter was safe for flight. I sabotaged the helicopter, I didn't know anyone else would be on there, I just wanted him out of the way."

I peered around the corner to see the expression on my grandmother's face.

"You're lying, We were all supposed to be on that plane ride! You were counting on my jealousy to force me to join him whether he liked it or not!"

There was fear in her eyes.

"Money can't have been your only motivation all of these years, why us? I thought you were Derek's childhood friend. You may as well tell me before I send you to jail."

Cliff moved in closer until he was directly in front of her face.

"He was no *friend*, he stole my idea for the company and profited off of it, he became rich while I was left humiliated; friend's don't serve other friend's. He used me and kept me close thinking I would take it lying down, It was my idea that led him to developing the technology that made him millions. I said that they should invent a way to operate on people without having to cut them open, and what was his great invention? Just that!"

This man was utterly twisted.

Jean stood up tall staring deep into his soulless eyes.

"You may have put an idea into Derek's head but he was the one who invented the technology, he earned every penny that he made and still let you

in as his personal adviser and trusted friend, a mistake which cost him his life. I fought with him when he gave you this job, he wanted you to be Vice President of his company but I convinced him you were only suited to serve."

Jean had noticed my presence and was clearly trying to aim Cliffs rage towards her and not me. There was a mirror behind them on the wall, just as I glanced into it I noticed Cliff had spotted me, I hid behind the statue again but it was too late he swiftly came to where I was standing.

He threw Jean to one side before grabbing me by my shoulders and thrusting me against the wall.

"You little brat, you are the cause of all of this, if you hadn't come to England I would've still been getting away with it. I regret ever finding you for that old wench, I knew where you were the whole time and I enjoyed seeing her suffer thinking you were lost. If I didn't need you around I'd never have brought you here. I guess now we'll have to do things the hard way."

I could barely get my voice out due to the way he had me pinned down.

"So why did you finally tell her where I was then?"

Cliff smirked with evil delight.

"I found the will of course."

He replied snidely.

He seemed to take enjoyment in being the one with all the secrets.

"I wanted you around to steal your inheritance, if the old woman dies guess who gets her estate. Sentimental old fool, I soon twisted the knife enough to get her to cause a rift between you both. I thought it would be enough for her to change the will, I gave her the idea to fake her death so that you would all hate her but you had to try to get proof. You had me on camera sneaking into the old study so I wiped your footage, thanks to my own set of recording equipment I picked up an odd reading from your room and checked it out. You thought you were pretty sneaky, you little rat."

It would have been better if he had remained silent, I had always wondered what he sounded like but now I wished that I would never hear his voice ever again.

With that last confession Grandma came up behind Cliff and whacked him over the head with a vase.

"Come on Abigail, let's get out of here, we need to call the police."

We fled from where Cliff was now lying unconscious, we only made it to the top of the stairs as Jean was getting tired of running.

"Grandma, let's use my mobile to ring the police."

I held out my phone and started to dial.

"ARGH!"

The world was spinning. I felt disoriented while the whole Mansion turned upside down. I'm not sure if I was in pain or not, or what was happening but the room had turned black I felt myself thud onto the floor shortly after jolting up and down violently but I now couldn't move. I heard footsteps on the ground faintly, then the sound of a door opening, finally slamming shut but that was it; the blackness turned into a bright white until I could hear and see nothing at all.

To be continued...

Printed in Great Britain
by Amazon